THE
PLANETOID
OF
AMAZEMENT

Mel Gilden

THE PLANETOID OF AMAZEMENT

HarperCollins*Publishers*

The Planetoid of Amazement
Copyright © 1991 by Mel Gilden
Printed in the United States of America. For information address
HarperCollins Children's Books, a division of HarperCollins Publishers,
10 East 53rd Street, New York, NY 10022.
Designed by Andrew J. Rhodes III
1 2 3 4 5 6 7 8 9 10
First Edition

Library of Congress Cataloging-in-Publication Data
Gilden, Mel.
The Planetoid of Amazement / by Mel Gilden.
  p.   cm.
Summary: Following strange instructions that come in the mail,
fourteen-year-old Rodney meets two aliens who are collecting
artifacts for an intergalactic museum, the House of Amazement on
Hutzenklutz Station.
ISBN 0-06-021713-8. — ISBN 0-06-021714-6 (lib. bdg.)
[1. Science fiction. 2. Humorous stories.] I. Title.
PZ7.G386Pl 1991   91-7261
[Fic]—dc20   CIP
                                                              AC

For Joe Humbert.
Because of the adventures.

CONTENTS

THE PLANETOID OF AMAZEMENT

1
Anything Can Happen

Rodney Congruent lived in a big museum and didn't like it. With his eyes closed, he carefully descended the stairs to breakfast carrying his schoolbooks in one hand and his black pebbled kazoo case in the other. With each step, his kazoo case banged against his leg. His eyes were closed because he didn't want to look at the stuff around him. Unless he kept his eyes closed, not looking was impossible, because stuff was everywhere. He'd seen all of it hundreds of times.

On the walls were paintings, enlarged photographs, and framed letters. Some of the pictures were of a man who wore a leather jacket, leather flight helmet, tall black boots, and pants that flared at the hips. He had a chin like a brick. In most pictures, this guy held a squat brown jar of a breakfast drink called "Chocolatron" as if he'd won it. All the other pictures were of some woman who had a paper bag over her head and a pair of milk cartons strapped to her back. She stood with her fists on her hips, a noble tilt to her paper bag.

The man in the flight outfit was Captain Conquer,

and the woman with the paper bag was the Tuatara. They were both heroes not only of the world at large, but of Rodney's parents in particular. When his parents had been kids, a series of docudramas about Captain Conquer had been on TV, and the Tuatara had been featured in her own comic book. Both presentations had supposedly been based on truth. Rodney was unsure how much of the stories had been invented, and his parents did not seem very clear on this themselves.

Only two things were certain: The first was that Rodney's father was the famous Watson Congruent, who had helped Captain Conquer save the Earth from the Puddentakers' plan to turn the atmosphere into cherry Jell-O. The second was that Rodney's mother was the former Pennyperfect Lieberman, who for years had been the Tuatara's able assistant. But all that was a long time ago, before Rodney was born.

The mantel over the fireplace held statues of Captain Conquer and the Tuatara; some of them were solid, others had once held shampoo, bubble bath, or children's vitamins. End tables acted as landing pads for models of the captain's ship, the *Great Auk*, and both of the Tuatara's ships, the *Flying Pterodactyl* and the *Mitzenmacher 260*.

Scattered among the statues and the models were mementos of the more famous adventures the two heroes had had: replicas of microbrains from the Penguin star, cheese-blight-shooting ray guns that had been prizes in jars of Chocolatron, and even a leather helmet that Mr. Congruent claimed had been worn by the captain himself.

The framed letters were from mayors and presidents, grateful for what Captain Conquer or the Tuatara had done. Sometimes Rodney's parents were mentioned by name.

Rodney was almost at the bottom of the stairs when Mrs. Congruent rushed by him, and against his will he opened his eyes. His mother was a handsome woman who had short silvery hair cut close, like a helmet, against her head. Her gray jumpsuit showed no wrinkles. She called out, "Have you seen my decoder ring, Rodney?" and didn't wait for an answer.

Rodney himself was a hefty kid with a head of brown hair that was more curly than he liked. Just as well his mom had hustled on. *He* didn't know where her old decoder ring was. He didn't want to know. He wished all the decoder rings in the world would disappear.

When Rodney arrived in the breakfast room, eyes open, and set his books and kazoo on the table, Mrs. Congruent was there, listening to Rodney's father say, "The decoder was on your dresser last night, next to your hyperspanner." Mr. Congruent was an older,

5

rounder version of his son, though he had less hair. He was dressed more or less like Captain Conquer. Because of the warm sunlight falling in through the tall windows, his leather flight jacket hung open. "Ah," said Mrs. Congruent. "I must have put them both into the toolbox." She marched from the room.

"If she can't find it," Mr. Congruent said, "I guess we can share mine." He tore open a paper packet and poured brown grainy powder into a mug of hot water before him. The smell of hot chocolate bloomed in the round room. "Have some Chocolatron, Rodney?"

Chocolatron had been Captain Conquer's favorite drink—he had made it famous. To Mr. and Mrs. Congruent it represented their exciting pasts, their moments of noisy fame. Rodney doubted if either of his parents would bother with Chocolatron otherwise. It was basically for kids.

"No thanks, Dad," Rodney said. He never drank Chocolatron, but his parents were hopeful he would start. Rodney was honest enough to admit that he was jealous of them. They'd both had adventures, while he had never done anything more exciting than play the kazoo in the Raff Street Junior High School orchestra. He liked playing the kazoo, but it wasn't the same as saving the planet.

The problem was that he was untested in the heroics department. He might be fine. But what if he couldn't hack it? What if, when the time came for bold action or daring escapes, his nerve failed him, or his cleverness, or his strength? Unthinkable. Yet here he was thinking it. The uncertainty was making him crazy.

Rodney said, "Wouldn't things be a lot simpler if the Chocolatron business reports weren't in code?"

"True, but most of us feel that Captain Conquer would have wanted them that way. Tradition is worth the bother of decoding." Mr. Congruent sipped his Chocolatron and said, "I mixed some Chocolatron with my oatmeal this morning."

"Hm," said Rodney.

"Well," Mr. Congruent went on enthusiastically, "I thought I'd present my idea at the sales conference. What do you think?"

"Sure, Dad."

"What's the matter, Rodney? That business with the adventures again?"

Rodney shrugged. How could his father understand?

"We'll be gone a few days at the sales conference."

"I'll be okay."

"I know that. You're a responsible lad. But just think, while we're gone you might have an adventure."

"Sure."

"You never know what might set one off. When my father gave me this Official Captain Conquer Signet Ring for my thirteenth birthday, I had no idea that it would plunge me into the adventure of my lifetime." He chuckled as he turned his hand, showing off the big, klunky ring for the umpteenth time. "Boy, was I one naive kid."

His parents were always pointing out possible adventures to Rodney. Anything could trigger them: a flat tire, getting lost ("You're not lost till you're out of gas!"), a wrong number on the telephone, sirens in the night, meetings with unknown relatives who suddenly turned up. Each event had been interesting, but not one of them had led to a real adventure. It was no use his parents being jolly.

Rodney said, "An adventure would be swell, yeah. But I don't think I'll ever have one. Those days are gone."

"You never know what might set off an adventure." Mr. Congruent said again. "Anything can happen."

Mrs. Congruent returned to the breakfast room and began to make herself a hot cup of Chocolatron. "I found the ring," she said. "Right in the toolbox next to the hyperspanner." She shook the hand with the ring on it in their direction.

When she sat down, she said, "I heard you practicing this morning, Rodney. You're getting better and better on that kazoo."

"Maybe I inherited Granddad's talent along with the

instrument." Rodney shook his head.

"What's the problem?" Mrs. Congruent said.

Rodney shrugged.

"He wants an adventure," Mr. Congruent said.

"I like the kazoo. Really, Mom."

Mrs. Congruent shook her head. "So you haven't had an adventure. You're just a kid, Rodney. You're not dead yet."

I might as well be, Rodney thought.

After breakfast, Rodney collected his books and his kazoo and left his parents at the table synchronizing their watches. When he opened the front door to leave for school, a man was standing there, his finger poised over the doorbell button. The man was dressed like Captain Conquer.

"Mom, Dad," Rodney called. "Your ride is here."

The man at the door helped them gather together their luggage and their briefcases and their lap-top computers. Rodney tried to help too, but the man treated him as if he were a piece of furniture that was just in the way.

As if it were the worst thing that could happen in the universe, the man said, "We'll be late for the plane," and hustled Mr. and Mrs. Congruent out the door. Rodney barely had a chance to say good-bye.

As Mr. Congruent was pulled out the door, he called after Rodney, "Anything can happen!"

9

"Right," Rodney said. He watched the man load his parents into a limousine shaped like Captain Conquer's mighty stratoship, the *Great Auk*. It pulled away from the curb with a roar.

Rodney stood at the door. Sometimes he imagined himself aboard a fancy ship like the *Great Auk*. Other times he wondered why he bothered.

Anything could happen, Rodney thought, but mostly it was just the same old stuff over and over again. He sat on the same old bus, swaying to its familiar rhythm. His books were in his lap, along with the electronic kazoo in its black pebbled case. He wasn't paying much attention to the world around him. It would take at least twenty minutes for the bus to creep through the morning Raff Street traffic to his school.

A fat guy huffed as he sat down in the empty seat next to Rodney. The guy was dressed in striped denim bib overalls and a railroad engineer's hat. His labored breathing sounded like a soft, tiny train whistle. Could this be the start of something big? Rodney watched carefully, feeling his every nerve tuned to any suggestion that the guy was about to ask him for help with some bizarre problem. But no. The guy got off two stops later and left nothing behind.

More of nothing happened after that. He rode the bus a little farther, then got off at school.

It was spring and everybody was a little crazy with its soft promises. School would be over in a month or so. Kids and teachers could see what Mr. Congruent persisted in calling "the light at the end of the tunnel." Despite his problem, Rodney felt pretty good. He carefully skirted a crowd of jocks who were horsing around, and went to sit with his friends.

"Morons," said Waldo, looking up from his nuclear physics book and gesturing with his head in the direction of the jocks; at the moment they were experimenting with shoving each other backward over the lunch benches. Waldo himself would never be a jock. He was enormously tall and thin. The black stuff on his head was more like toothbrush bristles than hair, and it stood up, Waldo said, because he'd once been struck by lightning. Rodney had never believed the lightning story. Waldo knew that and he didn't seem to mind.

Rodney made it through first-period gym class without offending his instructor too much. Second period was math, which he really kind of enjoyed, mostly because the teacher used to be a big-band singer; with spring in the air, it was not difficult convincing her to sing songs instead of teach math.

Third period was orchestra. Mr. Weinschweig taught the class in a bungalow away from the other buildings so that regular classes wouldn't be disturbed by all the noise of junior high school kids trying to make music.

The inside of the bungalow was shabby but friendly. The tile floor was faded and badly scuffed. The walls needed a new coat of green paint. In one corner was Mr. Weinschweig's desk. It was as old as anything else in the room, and it was piled high with sheet music. Though Mr. Weinschweig was not a little guy, when he sat at his desk he was hidden by the sheet music except for his bald head and maybe the top of his tortoiseshell glasses.

Mr. Weinschweig nodded to Rodney when he entered the bungalow, then went back to scribbling notes on music paper. It was no secret that Mr. Weinschweig was writing a symphony.

The thing that only Rodney knew, because Mr. Weinschweig had admitted it during a kazoo lesson, was that he'd been composing the first movement for the past fourteen years, since about the time Rodney had been born. He was always changing things— sometimes little tiddles, sometimes vast melodies. "I want it perfect," Mr. Weinschweig had told him. Maybe. But the result was that no one had ever heard one note of Mr. Weinschweig's symphony. Maybe it was great. Maybe it was rotten. Probably nobody would ever know.

A lot of kids were already in the bungalow warming

up by running their instruments up and down lopsided scales and playing bits of popular songs. The violins outnumbered everybody else, but the trumpets were the loudest. Once in a while the kid who played the drums would beat out a riff. The resulting chaos sounded like some of the overly modern music Rodney had heard on the radio.

Rodney sat down and plugged in his kazoo to conserve the battery power. He hummed into the kazoo and made a sound like a flying bee. He made the bee hum scales, adding to the confusion around him. Generally, Rodney wasn't much of a team player, but he liked playing in the orchestra. It was fun being in the middle of all that loud organized sound and seeing how all the parts fit together. As a matter of fact, Rodney's kazoo was one of the few highlights in his otherwise bleak life. Give him a kazoo and an empty room, and he could invent concerts that always got a standing ovation.

Pretty soon Mr. Weinschweig walked to the front of the room and began to conduct. If you took into account that they were just a junior high school orchestra, they sounded pretty good. They played the "Latvian Sailor's Dance" (traditional) and the "Robin Hood Overture" by Rooski-Pedruski. Mr. Weinschweig sometimes got so carried away that he closed his eyes and pretended he was playing an invisible violin with his baton. It was all pretty entertaining.

Orchestra class always seemed the shortest one of the day, and pretty soon it was time for the students to put away their instruments.

While Rodney swabbed out his kazoo with a rag of old T-shirt, he thought, So much for adventure. So much for excitement.

The house was empty when Rodney got home. After a moment he remembered that his parents were at the Chocolatron sales conference.

Just as well. He felt like being alone. After he put his books and his kazoo away, he picked up a stack of letters from the floor in front of the front door and sorted through them.

His parents must have been on some funny lists. They got advertisements from some magazines that wanted to make them millionaires, and from others that wanted them to "discover the romance of collecting antique slot machines"; from manufacturers who wanted to sell them Chocolatron scoops, from societies dedicated to the UFO method of tax preparation. Each envelope said something like YOU CAN'T AFFORD TO PASS UP THIS OPPORTUNITY! Or SAVE THE UNIVERSE. SAVE YOURSELF! Or even YOU MAY ALREADY BE IMMORTAL AND NOT EVEN KNOW IT!

That was why when Rodney saw an envelope with a headline written in curlicues and dots and splashes of color, he didn't think much of it. He guessed you were supposed to wonder what all that fancy art meant, and tear open the envelope in a sweat of curiosity. Like a lot of the other advertising, it was for his dad, but instead of it being typed or printed, the address was written in the scraggly longhand of a little kid. It was one curious package, all right. Rodney had to give the advertiser that.

He sat down with a plastic bag full of cherries and waited for his mom or dad to call in and ask about the mail.

2

Yellow Stickers

Rodney tried something with the cherries he'd once seen a cousin do. This cousin had a real talent for putting a whole cherry in one side of his mouth, and without seeming to stop for anything, roll a pit out the other side of his mouth. Rodney got the hang of it after a while, but by that time he had tracks of juice on his chin. He decided that he was too grown-up for this kind of thing and put the cherries away.

He'd just begun his math homework (everything they hadn't done in class because of the singing, they had to do for homework) when the phone rang.

While grumbling about being interrupted, Rodney leaped down the stairs and grabbed the phone on the third ring.

"Hello?"

"Hello, Rodney? This is your father."

"Oh yeah. I recognize the voice."

They both chuckled at the familiar little joke.

"So," said Rodney, "how's the conference?"

"My idea about putting Chocolatron into oatmeal went over very big."

"That's nice."

"You don't sound so good. Everything okay?"

Rodney was fine. He just wasn't about to get excited about Chocolatron. He said, "Sure. Do you want to hear about the mail?"

Mr. Congruent did. Rodney read him the copy on each envelope, and only one of them interested Mr. Congruent at all. He'd heard all the other pitches before. He said, "Open the one with the weird writing on it."

"Looks like more advertising to me," Rodney said.

"Yeah, but for what? Think about it."

Rodney didn't have to think about it. It was advertising. He put the phone down and tore open the envelope. He pondered the contents until he heard a tiny voice coming from the phone.

"Yeah, Dad. Sorry. I was just looking at the stuff in the envelope."

"Don't keep it to yourself, Rodney. What is it?"

Rodney said, "There's a pad of small yellow stickers, each about an inch square." He dropped the pad back into the envelope and took out a sheet of paper. "And this," he said, "looks like instructions."

"*Looks* like instructions?"

"Well, there are no words. Just pictures. Like the directions you get with a Japanese radio."

Excitedly, Mr. Congruent asked him what the instructions were.

"It looks," said Rodney, "as if they want you to tear

off a sticker and stick it on your forehead."

A moment later, Mr. Congruent said, "Go ahead."

"Go ahead? You mean you want your only son to just go ahead and stick this thing—which may be full of exotic skin poison—on his head? Just like that?"

"It's not poison, Rodney. It's an adventure."

Well, here it was. His big chance. He studied the instruction pictures over and over again, as if they could somehow tell him more. There was no way to know how dangerous applying a sticker might be. Was this how his parents had started? Had they been as uncertain about their futures as he was? Had their hearts beat as loudly? Had they sweated as much? Rodney could hear himself breathing into the telephone.

"Listen, Rodney. If somebody wanted to murder any of us with an exotic poison, they could just have put the poison in the paper the instructions were printed on. You'd already be a goner."

Rodney nodded.

"Are you nodding, Rodney?"

"Yeah, Dad, I'm nodding."

"Besides, any adventure involves an element of risk. That's one of the things that makes it an adventure. If I hadn't taken a chance, I might still be shoveling Chocolatron into the atomic furnaces of those crazy aliens."

"You're right, Dad. But these stickers are for you.

The envelope has your name on it." Rodney hated himself for saying this. His dad was pitching him the chance of a lifetime, and Rodney was lobbing it right back.

"You're my son. I've already had my adventure. I'm willing to give this one to you."

"Thanks." Right back in his court. Part of Rodney was horrified. A major part. But he knew if he didn't apply that sticker right now, he'd never do it. He'd never do anything except play the kazoo and maybe write the first movement of a symphony over and over again. And he'd continue to be jealous of his parents. More jealous, probably, knowing they'd succeeded and he hadn't. A terrible life.

Rodney set the telephone receiver on the table next to a folded cardboard model of the *Great Auk* and skidded his hands down his jeans to get rid of the sweat. He tore the top sticker off the pad. It came away easily. He looked at it. From this moment on, his life would be different. No more of this boring stuff. The excitement would never stop. He applied the sticker to his forehead and waited.

"Rodney?"

"Yes, Dad."

"Did you do it?"

"Yes, Dad."

"How do you feel?"

"About the same. I don't think these stickers do anything at all." Rodney was aware of his lighthearted tone. He felt as if he'd just taken off a backpack full of bricks.

"It's a strange sort of joke," Mr. Congruent said.

"Maybe it's not an adventure after all." Rodney was disappointed that this was such a relief.

"Don't give up so easily, Rodney. With adventures, you have to expect the unexpected. That's something else that makes an adventure."

"I suppose."

"If you have time, call me and your mother when something happens. You have the number?"

"If I have time?"

"Adventures sometimes come swiftly. You'll call?"

"Sure, Dad. If I have time."

"That's great. Anything else?"

They spoke for a few minutes more. Rodney asked Mr. Congruent to pass along his regards to his mom, and they hung up.

Rodney sat by the phone waiting to feel different. He felt a little nauseous, but that was probably because he'd eaten too many cherries. Nothing else. He was just some kid sitting next to a telephone with a square yellow sticker on his forehead. Rodney went back upstairs and started his math homework. When fifteen minutes had gone by, Rodney figured he'd given the adventure his best shot. Besides, the skin under the sticker was itching. He lifted his hand to pull the sticker off.

"*Yow!*" he cried. Rodney'd expected the sticker to just about fall off in his hand. But it didn't. Rodney pulled gently but firmly. The sticker stuck to his forehead as if it were a scab or something. He pulled harder. Nothing. He pulled hard enough to make his forehead hurt, but the sticker wouldn't come away.

Rodney rushed to the bathroom. He rubbed soap all over the sticker, then baby oil. Nothing would loosen it. He looked at himself in the mirror, breathing hard from excitement and from the exertion of trying to pull off the sticker.

Whoever sent these stickers had had their reasons. It could still be poisoning him, or twining through his nervous system, or who knew what? Rodney thought of calling his parents but decided not to. His father had given this adventure to him. It was up to Rodney to figure out what to do about it. Even if it killed him.

3

Under Rodney's Hat

Rodney tugged gently at the sticker while he finished his math homework. Entire minutes went by when he didn't even think about the sticker. It became just something to play with, like a callous or a hangnail. But at other moments he wondered when the sticker would begin to act, and what strange symptom he would notice first.

He wondered while he took his kazoo out of its case and plugged it in. He wondered while he set up his music stand and unfolded the music from the haircutting scene from Pastrami's *Samson and Delilah*. He wondered while he hummed the first notes at the top of the page into his kazoo. His wonder suddenly turned to horror.

Experimentally, he hummed into his kazoo again. At first, because the sounds he was making were so awful, he feared he'd forgotten how to hum. Then he decided that the sounds themselves were not awful. They were the same as always.

But now, unaccountably, in a matter of hours, his taste in music had changed. He hummed a few more notes into his kazoo, and the sound—which earlier that day had been so soothing—now put his teeth on edge. Itchy things crawled over his body.

He tried to remain calm but was not successful. Giving up the kazoo in order to have an adventure was not ever what he'd had in mind. Competing with his parents was silly, anyway. He didn't need to have an adventure just because they'd both had one. Of course, the yellow sticker didn't seem to be giving him a choice.

He frowned. And then with determination, Rodney began to hum into his instrument again. He concentrated on the music, but that didn't keep his skin from itching. He felt himself getting angry. By the time he'd finished the page, he was ready to tear phone books in half with his teeth.

Had the sticker changed his feelings only about kazoo music, or was it music in general? Rodney turned on the radio. A woman was singing a commercial about how everybody needed a credit card. The tune was trivial and the message insulting, but neither of them made Rodney itch. He turned off the radio and opened the "Latvian Sailor's Dance." The moment he began to play, jackhammers began pulverizing an old sidewalk inside his brain.

He sat in his chair sweating and breathing hard, the kazoo a dead weight in his hands. As far as he was

23

concerned, the sound of a kazoo was now fingernails on a slate, cats howling, and the whine of a dentist's drill all rolled into one. Rodney had never heard of a poison that made you hate kazoo music. There had to be more to it. Rodney would have to quit the orchestra. A yellow sticker did not seem like much to get in exchange.

Hoping to distract himself from the blackness closing in, Rodney put his kazoo away and went downstairs to watch TV.

By the time he had brushed his teeth, Rodney felt normal again. He studied the sticker in the bathroom mirror. It was the enemy. There had to be some way to defeat it. Maybe surgery was the only answer. Maybe electrolysis would work. The ads in the back of comic books said that electrolysis removed unwanted hair painlessly. Hair, stickers, what could be the difference? Rodney had no idea what electrolysis was, but he suspected it hurt more than the ads admitted.

He crawled into bed, stared at the blank ceiling for a moment, and decided he was being a goof. He switched on the light, got out of bed, and tried his kazoo once more. The vibration seemed to be shaking his brain loose. He got back into bed and turned out the light. He lay there for a while and was not even aware when he drifted into a dream.

In the dream Rodney had long slender hands covered with downy fur. If he crossed his eyes, he could see that his nose ended in a stubby snout. None of this bothered him; it all seemed normal. That all this weird stuff seemed normal *should* have bothered him, but this was a dream and it didn't. Rodney's dream personality seemed a lot like the personality he had while he was awake. He had a job to do, something a little vague—dreamlike—and he watched out for himself, but he was basically a good person who had no desire to hurt anybody.

Still, some things in the dream did upset him. He was far from home and had been roving for a long time, searching for something evil. In the dream the evil thing was a dirty brown blob that writhed and pulsated. It frightened Rodney even as it fascinated him. The evil thing had something to do with his job. Memories of adventures involving strange machines and stranger creatures did not excite him, but the longing to complete the job colored everything else like a thin gray fog.

Across the room, which seemed to be made of metal, was a creature three times his size. The creature looked like a bear that was wearing a utility belt around his middle and a small stool over his head as if it were a space helmet. The legs hung front and back and the rungs of the stool rested on the creature's shoulders. He and the bear seemed to be having a spirited discussion.

Whoever or whatever Rodney was, he liked and trusted the bear, though he thought the bear was kind of a goof with no serious goals or ideas. Like an uncle who showed up with presents from Outer Mongolia, bought everybody the biggest ice cream sodas they'd ever seen, stayed up all night eating cheese puffs and watching Marx Brothers movies on TV, and then went away, leaving your head swimming.

The bear turned around and adjusted one of the controls that covered the wall.

Then, as is sometimes the case in dreams, Rodney was suddenly somewhere else without quite knowing how he'd gotten there. He was outside under a black sky strewn with stars, walking across a field that extended as far as he could see. Huge alien machines stood at intervals on the field. The one nearest him had a sign floating in front of it. He thought he ought to be able to read the words on the sign, but he couldn't. That bothered him more than the fact that he was some animal and that he was consorting with bears who used tools. But it didn't bother him as much as what needed to be done with the evil thing.

After that the dream broke up into swirling alien machines and alien faces. One of the alien faces seemed to glow. It had enormous catlike eyes and two little holes for a nose. When it began to hum, Rodney needed to get away from it. Seeking refuge from the face and the terrible noise, he awoke to discover that his alarm clock was buzzing. He switched it off and fell back onto his bed. He enjoyed feeling more or less normal. Birds sang outside. Sunlight fell in through the window and landed silently on the floor in a brilliant yellow square. It was a relief to be at home.

He reached up and touched the sticker. Still there. He tugged on it and sighed when it pulled at the skin of his forehead. *An adventure for sure. Oh, yes.*

Rodney thought over the dream while he got ready for school. The dream was obviously trying to tell him something his brain was not prepared to understand. Maybe the sticker was some kind of training device. Training for what? By whom? The possibilities were mind-boggling, and he was perfectly willing to let his mind be boggled. But the explanation had better be good. He hoped he wasn't giving up his kazoo for just any wimp adventure.

He was about to walk out the front door when he remembered that the sticker was still in the middle of his forehead. Teachers and fellow students would, no doubt, ask embarrassing questions.

He opened the closet and studied the hats that

hung inside the door. Hanging there was another Captain Conquer leather flying helmet and a paper bag with holes for the eyes and mouth—the traditional headgear of the Tuatara. Also, there was a top hat with a card stuck into the band. The card said "In this style, 10/6." Farther along were a fedora, a slick yellow rain hat, and a shapeless knit thing you could pull down over your ears when the weather turned cold.

The knit hat would have been perfect, but the weather was too warm and he would have attracted suspicion. Rodney took the fedora and closed the closet door so that he could look at himself in the mirror on the other side. If he pulled the brim down far enough, he couldn't see the sticker. Not very well, anyway. If it was good enough for Humphrey Bogart, thought Rodney, it was good enough for him.

The bus ride wasn't so bad. Nobody cared whether or not a kid wore a hat. But once he got to school, he was not so lucky. He hadn't taken two steps onto the playground when he was stopped by Mr. Trowsinger, a stoop-shouldered, white-haired old guy who taught history.

"No hats in school," Mr. Trowsinger said in his feathery old voice.

"I have sort of a medical problem," Rodney said.

Mr. Trowsinger folded his arms, waiting. He'd been

teaching history since before Rodney was born, and he'd heard everything. Twice, maybe.

Rodney removed his hat, and Mr. Trowsinger bent to get a close look at the sticker. He lifted a hand and said, "May I?"

"Of course."

As gently as if he were touching the wing of a butterfly, Mr. Trowsinger tugged at the sticker. When it didn't come off, he grunted and crossed his arms again.

"It's feeding medication into my bloodstream. Through my skin."

"You have a note from your parents?"

"My parents are away at a Chocolatron sales conference."

"I see."

Mr. Trowsinger seemed to buy what Rodney was selling. He took Rodney to his classroom and wrote a note giving him permission to wear a hat in school until the sticker came off. Rodney was delighted with the note. It made everything else a lot easier. For one thing, it gave him an excuse to sit out gym class in the bleachers. His math teacher made a joke about hats and detectives, but otherwise left him alone. Mr. Weinschweig didn't seem to care one way or another.

When nobody was looking, Rodney stuffed tiny bits

of Kleenex into his ears. A pretty girl in a business suit sat down next to him and nodded in his direction. She was Nutti Phil, the second kazoo. The Kleenex didn't do much good. When Nutti hummed into her kazoo to warm up, it was all Rodney could do not to pull the vicious thing out of her mouth.

Mr. Weinschweig began to conduct; Rodney put his kazoo to his mouth, but he did not play. He gritted his teeth and tried not to listen to Nutti playing next to him. To Rodney, her playing sounded like somebody cutting sheet tin with an electric saw. The rest of the orchestra sounded just fine. He barely managed to get through the class without jumping around and tearing out his hair.

Fourth period was history. Mr. Trowsinger just nodded at Rodney when he came in wearing the hat. The period after that was lunch.

Waldo was reading a chemistry book when Rodney sat down on the bench next to him. As Rodney took a peanut butter sandwich from a plastic bag, Waldo glanced at him, nodded, and went back to his book. "Nice hat," he said.

"Thanks," Rodney said. "Want to see what's under it?"

Waldo closed his book on a finger and contemplated Rodney. "I've seen your head," Waldo said.

Rodney showed him the sticker and told him the

whole strange story. "I really miss the kazoo." He sighed and brushed crumbs from his lap. He said, "The funny part is that I'm scared of two opposite things. On the one hand, I'm scared that the sticker is the beginning of an adventure. I don't know if I can handle it."

"You can handle it."

"How do you know?"

"You're handling it already."

"Huh," said Rodney, feeling a little better and enjoying the feeling while he chewed. But the realization came to him that adventures always got bigger, never smaller. The confident feeling went away.

"What's the other thing you're scared of?"

Rodney swallowed and said, "I'm scared that these stickers are just some crazy advertisement for glue, not the beginning of an adventure at all. I'll end up like Mr. Weinschweig, writing the same movement of a symphony over and over again because I'm scared to continue. End up being jealous of my parents forever and hating myself because I know it's all my fault. And not even having the comfort of the kazoo anymore."

"*Would* it be all your fault?"

Rodney shrugged. His mood was gray and foggy. He'd felt like that before, just recently, though he couldn't quite remember when.

Waldo pulled on the sticker gently, as Mr.

Trowsinger had earlier. "And they call *me* weird," Waldo said.

Rodney put the hat back on and chewed his peanut butter sandwich.

Without looking up, Waldo said, "I can get it off for you."

"How?"

"Science," Waldo said mysteriously.

They planned to meet in the boys' bathroom after school. At that hour, nobody was likely to bother them.

The boys' bathroom was down a short flight of steps. It was cold and full of chemical and biological smells. A light scent of cigarette smoke hung over the stalls. Waldo was studying himself in the mirror when Rodney came in. "We're alone," Waldo said. "I checked."

"Good. What are you going to do?"

Waldo took a short, very sharp knife from his backpack and Rodney stared at it in horror. "That doesn't look very scientific to me."

"I use this knife in biology class. Surgery is very scientific."

"Don't touch me with that. You use it to cut up worms and frogs and stuff."

"Get a grip, Rodney. I sterilized it before I came

down here. Besides, I'm not going to cut you. Just the sticker."

Rodney looked at Waldo dubiously. Just how badly did he want the sticker removed? It might fall off by itself that evening. On the other hand, it might be a permanent exhibit on Rodney's forehead for years. "All right," he said.

"Come over here, then."

Rodney walked to Waldo and put his books and kazoo case on the floor. "Try to slice it off without killing me," Rodney said.

Waldo grunted as he studied Rodney, an artist studying an empty canvas. He held up the knife and leaned closer. Rodney closed his eyes. He felt Waldo tugging on the sticker. "What's going on?"

"This isn't paper," Waldo said. "It doesn't cut."

Rodney started to shake his head but Waldo commanded him to hold still. "I'll try slicing off a corner."

There was the tugging again, and suddenly Rodney felt dizzy. The floor opened away from him, and he fell toward the ceiling. He grabbed onto Waldo and held on tight. "Hey, watch it, man," Waldo said.

They stood like that for a minute while gradually the disorientation went away. The floor and the ceiling rotated back to their proper places. Rodney opened his eyes. "This isn't going to work," Rodney said. "That thing has probably welded itself to my nervous system."

"Maybe so." Waldo sounded disappointed. "What are you going to do?"

"I'm going to put on this hat and take the bus home. What about you?"

"Yeah," Waldo said. "I never claimed that science knew everything."

At home the mail was the usual mix of bills and advertisements. One letter was selling guided trips to Tierra del Fuego. Another was offering him the chance to win five million dollars if he bought some designer luggage featuring the signature of Rocky Smith, Space Commando. A third advertised a foolproof way to survive the coming invasion of killer ants "for fun and profit."

Then Rodney saw the envelope. It was like the one addressed to his father the day before, like the one in which the pad of stickers had come.

But the interesting thing was, the exciting thing was, the thing that meant adventure was that where yesterday the headline on the envelope had been just so many chicken scratches, today he could read the chicken scratches as if they were English. Whatever else it was doing, Rodney had the suspicion that the sticker was also doing its job. For a moment, the loss of the kazoo seemed a little less important.

The headline said VISIT THE PLANETOID OF AMAZEMENT (RTE. HUTZENKLUTZ STATION).

Rodney knew that he was really reading the writing and not just pretending, because every time he looked at it, it said the same thing. He shook the envelope. Something was inside. Whether it was more stickers or something else Rodney could not tell. He wanted desperately to open the envelope, but it was addressed to his father in that same unsophisticated handwriting. Rodney would have to wait. He sat down on the steps.

After a while, it occurred to him that he was missing an important opportunity to check himself. He pawed through the papers on the telephone table and found the envelope from the day before. He could read these chicken scratches too! They said EXCITING FREE OFFER! YOU MAY HAVE ALREADY WON A TRIP TO THE PLANETOID OF AMAZEMENT! USE YOUR STICKER TODAY!

No doubt about it now. The sticker had taught him how to read this weird language. But unless the Planetoid of Amazement was something really special, not just a video-game arcade or something, it was not much of a trade for playing the kazoo.

Time walked by in no particular hurry. He picked up and shook a gray plastic box that had the Captain

Conquer wings stamped on it and a metal antenna you could pull out till it was a few feet long. The communicator box rattled and made a twanging sound. Inside, Rodney knew, were wires and springs and electronic blobs. When he'd shown the inside of the communicator to Rodney, Mr. Congruent had said, "I think it would work even now if it received the right signal." Rodney had considered this unlikely, but he'd said, "Sure, Dad." Rodney put down the communicator and picked up a wooden model of the *Mitzenmacher 260*, which he zoomed through the air.

When the phone rang, Rodney jumped and put down the model. "Hello?"

"How are you, Rodney?"

"Okay, Mom. How are you and Dad and the conference?"

"The new Chocolatron advertising campaign is very exciting."

"Hm," said Rodney.

"Yes," his mother went on, "I always liked 'It's atom powdered,' but most of the delegates think that slogan is old-fashioned. They like 'Chocolatron: a blast from the past.'"

"Hm."

"That's what *I* said."

"Uh, did Dad tell you about the strange envelope with the stickers inside?"

"He certainly did. It was very exciting. Any adventures to report?"

"Not exactly." Rodney told his mother what had been going on, about the dreams and the problem with the kazoo and all.

"This is very good," Mrs. Congruent said.

"But what does it all mean?"

"You'll find out soon enough, I'm sure. That's the way adventures work."

"Dad got another one of those strange envelopes. Only now I can read what it says."

"The work of the sticker, of course. What does it say?"

"It says VISIT THE PLANETOID OF AMAZEMENT (RTE. HUTZENKLUTZ STATION)."

"Very interesting."

"The Planetoid of Amazement is probably a second-rate amusement park or a restaurant where they pay more attention to the video games than to the food."

"You believe that?"

"No."

"Have you opened the envelope yet?"

"No," Rodney said patiently. "It's addressed to Dad." That was a good excuse, anyway.

"If you want to, open the envelope, Rodney. I think your father would insist on it."

Rodney knew his mom was right. He no longer had a reason to avoid the inevitable. He held the receiver of the phone under his arm and sighed. With a mighty effort, he tore open the envelope. Inside was another instruction sheet and a foil packet. He held the packet up to the light and shook it, but still couldn't tell what was inside.

The instruction sheet showed one side of the packet being torn off, and whatever was inside being poured over the outline of a person. In the drawing, the stuff looked like sand. At the top of the sheet something was written in the funny language that Rodney could now read.

"Mom?" said Rodney into the telephone.

"Yes, Rodney?"

"There's a packet and some instructions. I don't know what's in the packet, but the instructions say GREETINGS, WATSON CONGRUENT. OPEN THE PACKET. THROW THE CONTENTS OVER YOURSELF AND GET A BIG SURPRISE.

"My husband has obviously been keeping secrets from me." Mrs. Congruent laughed and went on, "You must immediately do as the instructions suggest."

"We're talking adventure here, aren't we, Mom?" A hot wind rushed through Rodney's body. He felt as if he had the flu.

"I'm sure of it," Mrs. Congruent said.

"Okay, then," said Rodney. "Here I go."

Rodney put down the phone. He tore open the packet and poured the contents into his hand. Whatever it was looked like the kind of glitter a little kid would glue onto a homemade Mother's Day card. Judging by the strange properties of the sticker, this glitter probably was not as innocent as it looked.

With a sense that he was jumping off a cliff, he took a deep breath and threw the glitter over his head. As the glitter settled, the edges of each bit seemed to slice through the very fabric of reality. The world seemed to disintegrate around him.

Rodney's last thought before he was engulfed by darkness was that he'd neglected to hang up the phone.

4

Woman Flagging Down a Bus

Rodney did not move. Bits of somewhere else fell around him, and like puzzle parts the size of snowflakes, they built up Rodney's new location.

As far as he could tell, he was now inside the metal room he had seen in his dream the night before. The huge bear wearing the utility belt and the stool helmet was motioning to him in an incomprehensible way. Meanwhile, a kangaroo creature was rushing from place to place in the round room, obviously searching for something. Occasionally the kangaroo creature would look at him and at the bear and shake its head.

Rodney inhaled deeply and took in the cool air, which smelled faintly of machine oil. He was doing all right so far. He was a little afraid, but only a dope wouldn't be. Mostly, he was interested, curious, and ready to expect the unexpected. He looked around the room.

The walls were covered with buttons and gauges and small toggle switches. At one side of the room— you couldn't say that a round room had an end—was a single round window that seemed to be blank.

When Rodney walked over to look out the port-hole, what he saw surprised him, excited him, and made him more afraid. Outside, hanging among the powdering of stars, was the planet Earth, looking blue and serene, much as it did in Space Agency photographs. Everything and everybody he knew was down there. He was alone. All questions about his ability to handle an adventure were about to be answered. And there wouldn't be any last-minute rescues, not even if he needed one.

Rodney turned around when the bear said something that sounded like "Ompah! Veigh iz tzoo mere! Slignathi tzoo mere!" His voice was kind of a growl, pretty much what you'd expect from a bear.

The kangaroo answered, "Some tau!" and rushed around the compartment with even more determination. The kangaroo's voice was a surprise. It was the voice of a sweet young girl.

Rodney said, "What's going on? Where am I?"

The kangaroo cried, "Lerique! Lerique!" and handed the bear a white thing like a toothpaste tube.

The bear motioned Rodney closer, opened the tube, and squeezed out a column of clear jelly on the calloused black pad of a finger. He held up the finger to Rodney's forehead. Rodney flinched, then stood steady. The bear rubbed the jelly across the top of the yellow sticker, and seconds later the sticker fell away.

41

Rodney rubbed the itchy spot as the bear threw the sticker down what appeared to be a disposal chute.

The kangaroo held up a sheet of paper to Rodney. In the funny squiggles, it said IF YOU CAN READ THIS, WAVE YOUR HANDS! This was amazing! Evidently, the sticker was not a translator, but a teaching aid. It had actually taught him to read the alien language, perhaps permanently. Enthusiastically, Rodney waved his hands.

The kangaroo waved back at Rodney and then handed the bear a pad of blue stickers. As he tore one off and held it up to Rodney's forehead, Rodney wondered where he could get his own tube of that jelly. The bear applied the blue sticker.

"How's that?" the bear said.

"I can understand you fine," said Rodney. He wasn't even surprised. The activities of the past twenty-four hours had prepared him for something just like this. Rodney said, "What language are we speaking?"

The kangaroo said, "This is Mobambi, the interstellar trading language. But I want to introduce my boss. This," the kangaroo said with a flourish of one hand, "is Grubber Young, owner and operator of the House of Amazement on Hutzenklutz Station—sometimes known as the Planetoid of Amazement. You are aboard his ship, the Ship of Amazement. I am Drum, whom he employs as his finder."

"I am Rodney Congruent."

"Rodney?" said Grubber Young. He and Drum shared a worried glance.

"Sure. Rodney, son of Watson and Pennyperfect."

"Not Watson himself?"

"No. But I had his permission to open those envelopes, if that's what you're worried about."

"What a surprise!" Drum said, as if she were really bowled over by the news.

"That's nothing compared to how surprised I am that you know my father and his address."

"Nothing to be surprised about," said Grubber Young. He nodded to Drum. Drum pushed a button, and a ball of lightning fizzed briefly in a niche in the wall. When the lightning went away, Drum took a sheet of paper from the niche. Rodney was convinced that the sheet had not been there before. Drum said, "This is just a copy, of course," and handed the paper to Rodney.

Half of the paper was taken up with a simple outline drawing of a naked man and a naked woman. The other half of the paper was covered with line after line of squiggles. "What is this?" Rodney said.

"You've never seen it before?" Drum said.

"No."

Drum showed Rodney a thing that looked like a ballpoint pen. When Drum clicked the stem at the top, a cone of light came out of the end where the pen point would have been, and touched the paper. Wherever it touched, it magnified. Drum handed the magnifier to Rodney, and he played it over the squiggles.

Each little bunch of squiggles seemed to be a message of some sort. One said GREETINGS FROM PLANET EARTH. Another said WE'LL BE HOME FOR CHRISTMAS. A third was a complex mathematical equation followed by the words CAN YOU TOP THIS?

"I don't understand," Rodney said.

"Look here," said Grubber Young, and he aimed the magnifier at a squiggle farther down the page. There, in the same wiggly handwriting as had been on the envelopes, was the name WATSON CONGRU-ENT and the address of the Congruent home.

"Where did you get this?" Rodney said.

"Off a space probe."

"A space probe from Earth?"

"So we've been led to believe."

"Believe? By what? By who?"

"Take a look at these," Grubber Young said as he pointed to some rectangles along the bottom edge of the paper.

Rodney shone the magnifier onto the rectangles and saw that they were photographs of famous places all over the world. There was the Sphinx and the Eiffel Tower and the Great Wall of China and a lot more.

Grubber Young pointed at the Statue of Liberty and said, "That was the giveaway. Drum?"

Drum was ready with a postcard. She handed it to Grubber, who handed it to Rodney. On the postcard was a picture of the Statue of Liberty. But the picture was better than a photograph because it was three-dimensional, and the clouds moved and Rodney imagined that he could hear the ocean licking against the island where the statue stood. At the bottom, in Mobambi, it said LOCAL FOLK TRANSPORTATION ICON: WOMAN FLAGGING DOWN A BUS. *(Photo by Sak Nussemm, of Earth origin).*

"I see," said Rodney. He tried not to laugh. After all, it was possible that archeologists and anthropologists on Earth made mistakes about ancient cultures all the time. Nobody would ever know. "But I still don't understand how my address got on the side of that probe."

"It's *your* probe," said Drum, laughing. "*You* tell *us*."

Nobody spoke. Rodney could hear air moving through the ship like an endless breath. Somewhere, a relay snapped. Rodney needed to change the subject. He tapped the edge of the postcard on the palm of his other hand and said, "Where do you get postcards like this?"

"From the Starship Club," said Grubber.

"What's that?"

"It's a wonderful organization," said Drum. "They supply emergency interstellar service, sell insurance, and run a travel agency at cut rates. Grubber has been a member for years. They send us postcards like this all the time."

"But how did you find the Earth?"

Grubber said, "There are instructions." He pointed to a complex diagram between the naked man and the naked woman. Rodney shone the magnifier on it and saw that it had spectrum lines defining Earth's sun by its chemical composition, and all kinds of arrows and circles. Generally, the diagram looked like a map of a freeway interchange.

"You can see the probe leaving the third planet from the Sun," Drum said.

Rodney nodded, trying not to show his distress. Anybody who'd been awake during eighth-grade science class knew that the third planet from the Sun was Earth. And if they watched old science-fiction movies, they also knew that telling aliens the location of your home planet was generally a bad idea. Rodney couldn't change the fact that the aliens were here, but he didn't have to help them. At least not till he knew their intentions. Feeling like some kind of spy, he handed the postcard and the paper and the magnifier back to Drum and said suspiciously, "You figured out the location of the Earth and its sun from this?"

"Well, actually not us alone. The Starship Club helped us read the instructions." Drum opened her arms wide and cried, "Grubber just wanted to drop in and say hello."

"Well," said Grubber with self-importance, "we're here on business too."

Rodney folded his arms and said, "What sort of business?"

Grubber held up his hand, and from his utility belt he pulled something that might have been a timepiece. On it, Mobambi numbers changed rapidly. He used more clear jelly to remove Rodney's blue sticker. "Can you still understand me?" he asked.

Still suspicious, Rodney said, "I understand the words."

"Can't ask for better than that."

Rodney disagreed, but he said, "That blue sticker didn't take long to work. Is the yellow sticker that fast?"

"Give or take a few minutes," Drum said.

So Rodney had suffered the humiliation of wearing that sticker to school for no reason. He'd evidently been able to read that first envelope almost immediately, though he hadn't actually discovered what the sticker had done to him till the mail came the following day. Of course, he hadn't had any of that handy jelly, so maybe none of this mattered after all. He said "You still didn't tell me what your business here is."

"Absolutely right, kid." Like a carnival barker, Grubber pointed his finger in the air and declaimed, "The House of Amazement is a museum where people come to see artifacts from all across the galaxy." Grubber became more enthusiastic. "One can see flying objects, both identified and un. Probes, of course. We've got your satellites, your space suits and armor, your ray guns, your antimatter torpedoes, and your hyperdrives."

"Many of the things are so alien," Drum admitted, "we don't know what they are."

"And so?" said Rodney, waiting for the big revelation.

"And so," Grubber Young said as he shook the postcard of the Statue of Liberty in the air, "we came to pick up a few souvenirs."

5

The Invasion of Earth

"You'll never get away with this," Rodney said.

Grubber Young lowered the postcard. "Get away with what?" he said.

"You can't just walk in here and steal the Statue of—er—the *Woman Flagging Down a Bus.* We're not as backward as we look. Every country in the world has an air force. And there's the Space Agency." Rodney thought furiously. "And Starfleet Command will have something to say about it too."

Grubber and Drum fell all over each other laughing, which was an odd thing to see, Grubber being so much larger than Drum. When Grubber had caught his breath, he said, "You got us all wrong, kid. We're not the Slignathi, after all. Besides, people don't want to see stuff like the *Woman Flagging Down a Bus.* It's too highbrow. There's no market for it. Anyway, we're not here to steal."

"No?" said Rodney, unconvinced.

"No. Chances are we'll see something lying around that nobody wants. Fast-food burger wrappers are thought of as pretty exotic in some parts of the galaxy. If you have burger wrappers on Earth. I don't know, of course. Or we might buy some touristy stuff. You know, beads and trinkets. All kinds of tchotchkies. The marks at—er—the customers at the House of Amazement will be just as amazed."

"*Buy* touristy stuff? What will you use for money?"

"What about the magnifier? That must be worth something."

"You're going to sell magnifiers?"

"No, no. We're more into barter."

This was all wrong. Unless the universe was not only stranger than he'd imagined but sillier, Rodney could not believe anyone would come to Earth for fast-food wrappers. He'd have to find out all he could about these yahoos. Who knew what knowledge might be important when the invasion began? Rodney said, "All right. Say I believe you. Then what?"

"Then we visit your lovely planet."

"People will notice."

"No, they won't. We have the Slignathi's own ways. You'll see. But there is one thing we will have to do. Drum?"

Drum nodded and turned a section of wall on a pivot. On the other side was what looked like the high arched front of an old wooden radio. Drum turned a dial and a small lamp glowed weakly behind a yellow bar with numbers on it. By turning another dial, she was able to move a red line to the proper number. As she did this, static and hisses and a noise like someone kissing a rubber balloon came from the cloth-covered speaker. It seemed to Rodney that he could hear faint faraway voices speaking in English and in languages that he could not understand, not even with the help of the blue sticker.

Drum flicked a toggle upward, and something inside the machine began to grind. A moment later, a pad of red stickers stuck out of a slot like a tongue and fell into a large metal cup. The machine sighed to itself as if it had just laid an egg one size too big. As Drum shut off the radio and turned the wall around again, Grubber took the red stickers and said, "Here we are."

"More stickers?" Rodney said.

"Oh, these aren't for you. They're for us. So that we can understand your local tongue." Grubber chuckled. "Drum and I wearing red stickers is much more practical than giving blue stickers to everybody on your planet." He slapped a red sticker on his own forehead and one on Drum's forehead.

"Testing: one, two, three," Drum said.

"Sounds like English to me," Rodney said.

"Actually, it's not English at all, but a clever simulation. What matters is that we can understand each other perfectly." The perfection of their understanding delighted Drum.

"That's great, but will I still be able to understand Mobambi?"

"Of course," Grubber said in Mobambi.

Drum nodded and said, "These are the Mark IV stickers, after all. You wear them for a while and *gazornenplatz!* You're educated forever."

"Language isn't your only problem," Rodney said.

Grubber went on in English. "We know problems you haven't thought of, kid. Earth is not the first alien planet we've ever visited," Grubber Young said. "Now, you'd better get your seat belt on."

"You're landing on Earth?"

"Nothing to worry about," said Drum. "We land on planets all the time." She winked at Rodney.

Sure, Rodney thought. Just another notch on the old ray gun. What could he do to stop these guys? Sadly, he decided he'd come to the end of his rope. It was more important to save the planet than it was to continue pretending he could handle a situation that was rapidly escalating into an all-out interplanetary invasion. He needed to get to a phone. "Let's go to my house," Rodney said, hoping his bright tone wouldn't arouse suspicion. "You can meet my dad."

"Great idea," Drum said. Grubber agreed and adjusted some dials.

Rodney sat on one end of a couch while Grubber and Drum sat at the other end. They all buckled up with heavy-duty seat belts. The couch was comfortable and covered in a nice nappy brown material. From it all three of them could look out the porthole while Grubber and Drum fiddled with controls as they followed a checklist.

"Spaceman's luck!" cried Drum. Grubber Young pushed a button. With a roar of rockets, the ship fell out of orbit toward the Earth.

The Earth seemed to turn quickly as it rushed up toward them. Rodney felt no motion. He might as well have been sitting on the couch in his living room. He tried to remember everything the aliens did, every detail of the ride. Even if he lost the adventure to the military, he and his information might be planet Earth's only hope.

There was a snuffling noise, like a vacuum cleaner sucking dust off venetian blinds, as the ship fell through Earth's atmosphere and across the terminator into the night side of the planet. They dropped through clots of cloud and then empty air. The thunder of the rockets grew, then died suddenly. There was a small bump. All in all, Rodney had been on more exciting amusement-park rides.

Grubber made a big ceremony out of removing the red stickers from his forehead and Drum's. "Does this sound like English?" Grubber asked when he finished.

"Great," Rodney said. Aliens who could speak English struck him as *very* dangerous. Maybe they were spies as well as collectors.

Drum pulled a big lever, and a section of the wall unfolded in a way Rodney could not follow. The three of them were now standing at the top of a short wooden staircase. Rodney could see that they were in his backyard next to the avocado tree. He marched down the stairs, his hand resting lightly on the banister. His neck prickled at the thought that Grubber Young and Drum were right behind him.

Rodney didn't have a key to the back door, so they had to go around front. Before he turned the corner of the house, he glanced back for a look at Grubber Young's ship, the *Ship of Amazement*. Know your enemy. To his surprise, the outside was square. Its smooth white surface gleamed in the moonlight. More than anything else, the ship looked like a front-loading washing machine.

When he got around to the front of the house, the street was deserted, as it usually was at night. Rodney was disappointed to see that the arrival of the ship hadn't attracted a crowd. When he asked about that, Grubber said, "Nobody noticed us because, well, nobody noticed us. We use a reversed version of the magnifier to make the ship look as if it were the size of a dust mote."

"I didn't feel a thing."

"We didn't really shrink any more than those pictures really got bigger when you looked at them." Grubber winked at Rodney. "You see—we have everything covered."

"Slignathi smart," Drum said.

"Very impressive." Rodney loitered in front of the house for a while, admiring the cloudy sky and the sweetness of the night. He hoped that somebody would see them, notice that the Earth was being invaded, and sound the alarm. Nobody did. The street was deserted. Rodney felt a little better now that sounding the alarm was still up to him. It was all he had left as far as adventures went.

Casually, Rodney said, "So who are these Slignathi guys you keep talking about?"

"Scary guys," said Drum.

"Monsters from the Sid," Grubber said, and suddenly laughed.

"The Sid?" said Rodney.

"A legendary but real-sounding star system. The Slignathi are supposedly a nasty race whose members are masters of disguise and conquerors of many planets."

"Is that funny?" Rodney said.

"The thing is," said Grubber, his voice rising, "is that they don't exist! I've been all over this galaxy and never gotten any closer to the Slignathi than ghosts of old lukewarm rumors. Right, Drum?"

"It's a big universe," Drum said, and shrugged as she looked at the sky.

Grubber studied Drum for a moment.

Rodney said, "So why do you talk about them all the time?"

Grubber shrugged and said, "It's kind of like slang. You might say, 'I'll be a Slignathi's uncle.' Or 'Slignathi's luck,' or even, 'Is it real or is it Slignathi?'"

It occurred to Rodney that for all he knew, these guys could be Slignathi themselves.

Joshing, Grubber said, "So, are we going in or what?"

When they went in, Grubber had to bend over to get through the doorway.

Rodney gathered them in the living room, then backed away as he said, "You wait right here. I have to go do something."

He ran to the telephone at the foot of the stairway and saw the receiver was lying on the floor. And for some reason it was dead. Then he remembered with a shock that he'd been holding the receiver when he'd thrown the glitter over himself. No wonder the phone was dead. It had been off the hook for hours.

Rodney hung up the phone, but he couldn't wait around to see if that would bring back the dial tone.

Besides, he had a better, more private idea. He ran up the stairs. If he was lucky, Grubber and Drum would think he was going to the bathroom—if they had bathrooms where the aliens came from. He went to his parents' bedroom and shut the door.

On a table next to the bed was the Chocolatron Hotline. He'd been cautioned never to use it except on official Chocolatron business, but this was an emergency, and he was sure his parents would forgive him. Despite the seriousness of the situation, he felt a little silly using the hotline, because it looked like a jar of Chocolatron.

Rodney hunched over the hotline to block the sound, then lifted the lid and held it to his ear. A moment later a woman at the other end of the line said, "Chocolatron Hotline."

Rodney whispered into the jar.

"I can't hear you, sir."

In a husky stage whisper, Rodney said, "I need help. Earth is being invaded by aliens from space."

You never knew how an adult would react to an announcement like that, and Rodney never found out how the Chocolatron Hotline operator stacked up. A hairy hand pulled the lid from his grasp and Rodney spun around. The owner of the hairy hand was Drum. She shook her head and, as if disappointed in Rodney, said, "No, no, no."

As she settled the lid back onto the jar, Rodney heard somebody coming along the hall. It was Grubber Young, of course. He looked into the bedroom, saw Rodney and Drum, and chuckled. He said, "You're up to the Slignathi's own mischief, Rodney. I don't know what we're going to do with you."

Rodney didn't know either. But that chuckle of Grubber's had a sinister sound. Rodney stood there trying to show a brave front, but inside he was terrified.

6

The *Vagabond Lover III*

Rodney closed his eyes and said, "Do your worst."

"What?" said Drum.

"I tried to save my planet and I'm proud."

"Save it from what?" said Drum.

"Hey, open your eyes kid," Grubber Young said. "We're not as ugly as all that."

Rodney opened one eye. Drum and Grubber Young were standing there looking bewildered. Neither of them held a recognizable weapon. Neither of them acted angry. "If you guys think stopping me will make the Earth easier to invade, you're making a big mistake."

"Why doesn't anybody *trust* me?" Grubber said. "We're not going to invade the Earth!"

"We told you," Drum said, and laughed. "We're here to pick up new exhibits for the House of Amazement."

"Sure," said Rodney. "Like the *Woman Flagging Down a Bus*."

"Great Slignathi," said Grubber as he shook his head. "I told you. We're after wrappers, key chains, milk cartons—that sort of thing."

"Then why did you stop me from calling the . . . Air Force?"

Rodney flinched when Grubber put his big arm around his shoulder and walked him out of the bedroom and back along the hall. "Think about it, Rodney," Grubber said as they strolled. "We're aliens. A lot of people would think what you're thinking. We'd get into big trouble." Grubber steered him to the top of the stairs. Was he going to push Rodney down?

Rodney tried to wriggle loose and found it impossible. He said, "Why shouldn't I think what I'm thinking?"

"Think about it," Drum said.

Rodney had lost the thread of the conversation. He said, "Huh?"

Grubber let go of Rodney, and he backed away from the stairs. Grubber said, "Listen, kid: When you stuck one of those yellow stickers onto your forehead, you didn't just learn to read Mobambi and get a little introduction to the House of Amazement."

"Oh, no," Drum said, and waggled a finger at him.

Grubber went on, "Oh, no. You also got a condensed extract of Drum's mind. What does she think of me? What does she think of herself?"

Rodney remembered the things he'd felt in his

strange dream. Grubber Young was kind of a goof but harmless. Drum was a lot like Rodney except for her longing to find the evil thing. Rodney wondered briefly if she was after a Slignathi. But wouldn't that mean she wasn't one of them? Did they even exist? He said, "The sticker could have been lying."

"No way," Drum said. "You would have felt the lying just like you felt everything else. You can't lie with your mind and get away with it."

While Rodney was thinking about that, wondering if it were true, a key turned in the front-door lock downstairs and his parents came in carrying their luggage. They must have convinced the chauffeur that they could make it from the car to the house all by themselves. They looked a little beat.

Rodney and Drum shared a glance. Drum was serious for a moment, and then she smiled hopefully. Grubber was behind him, so Rodney didn't know what he was doing.

Many thoughts rushed through Rodney's mind in the few seconds before his parents looked up the stairs. Should he trust Grubber and Drum or should he attempt to get his parents to sound the alarm? Though it could be an entire fabrication, what they said about the sticker made sense. The person lying always knew he was lying, so the person reading his mind would always know, too. Also, Grubber and

Drum hadn't killed him when he'd attempted to use the hotline.

Nothing was certain, but Rodney decided to err on the side of adventure. His adventure. If he gave it up now, he'd always wonder if he could really finish it or not. He'd be jealous of his parents for the rest of his life. "Hi, guys," Rodney called.

Mr. and Mrs. Congruent blinked up at him from the foyer. Mr. Congruent said, "Rodney, my boy! Good to see you're safe. When your mother lost contact with you, we were curious to find out what happened."

"And a little worried, too," Mrs. Congruent said.

"That's why we came home from the sales conference early. Come help us carry our baggage upstairs, and tell us everything." Then Mr. Congruent and his wife saw Grubber and Drum, and they looked very surprised.

Mrs. Congruent, who was always better in social situations than Mr. Congruent, put on her company smile and said, "Rodney, won't you come down and introduce us to your friends?"

Rodney descended, Grubber and Drum right behind him. With uncertain pride, he said, "Mom, Dad, this is Grubber Young and his finder, Drum. Grubber is the owner and operator of the House of Amazement on Hutzenklutz Station, sometimes known as the Planetoid of Amazement. At the moment, his space ship, the *Ship of Amazement*, is parked in our backyard."

"Well, what do you know?" Mr. Congruent said. He sounded gratified, as if someone had just given him an expensive present. "Would you like some Chocolatron? It's atom powdered."

Mrs. Congruent set a hand on her husband's arm and said, "Not anymore, dear."

"That's right. Now it's a blast from the past." He shook his head.

"Why not?" said Grubber Young. He and Drum followed the Congruents into the breakfast room. Grubber took up an entire side of the table. Rodney and Drum shared a side. There was plenty of room for everybody. Mr. Congruent leaped up and went into the kitchen. Through the doorway, they could see him heating milk for the Chocolatron. Meanwhile, Mrs. Congruent made polite conversation with Grubber.

"We are delighted," Grubber said. "Our welcome on a new planet is not usually so cordial. People sometimes think they're being invaded." He and Drum laughed.

"Hey, it happens," Rodney said and laughed with them.

From the stove, Mr. Congruent said, "We have

more experience with adventure than most." He launched into the story of how he'd saved the Earth. Rodney had heard it before and was a little embarrassed. After all, the adventure his father had had when he was a kid couldn't sound like much to two beings from the other end of the galaxy.

But Grubber and Drum listened seriously, marveling out loud in all the right places. When Mr. Congruent was done, Drum said, "Those Puddentakers are bad news."

"Indeed," Grubber said. "You're well rid of them."

Mr. Congruent set out three big steaming mugs. Rodney looked at them with disgust. One was obviously for him. He didn't usually drink Chocolatron, but this seemed to be a special occasion. The stuff wasn't really bad, after all, and besides, somebody who could handle an adventure didn't complain when served one of the local drinks. Rodney blew gently on his Chocolatron while watching his father. He knew the time would come soon when it would be decided exactly whose adventure this was.

Rodney took a deep breath and said, "Dad, Grubber Young and Drum found a space probe with your name and address on it."

"What's this?" Mr. Congruent said. His wife looked at him with astonishment.

Grubber said, "Absolutely. Your name and address

were etched into a gold plate. That's why we're here. We've come to say hello." He pointed his finger at Mr. Congruent. Mr. Congruent looked at the finger for a moment, then pointed his finger at Grubber Young. Grubber hooked his finger around Mr. Congruent's and yanked on it a couple of times. Mr. Congruent yanked back. "We are pleased to meet you, Watson Congruent."

"You never told me about this, dear," Mrs. Congruent said.

"Well, I don't . . ." Mr. Congruent began. He shook his head and frowned. "Are you sure?"

From her kangaroo pouch, Drum took the copy of the gold plate and handed it to Mr. Congruent, along with the magnifier. Rodney's mom and dad studied the paper for a while, exclaiming over the photographs and the messages.

Mr. Congruent snapped his fingers and cried, "Of course. I remember now. After my experience with Captain Conquer and the Puddentakers, I became interested in science fiction. I went to a lot of science-fiction conventions. At one of them the Space Agency had a table where, for a small donation to the space program, you could write a short message on a sheet of paper. Later, the Space Agency people would use some photographic process to engrave your exact message on the side of a space probe. I thought it was just some publicity gimmick." He frowned again. "Now, what probe was it?"

They sat for a while, just drinking their Chocolatron. Rodney was glum. His chances of finishing this adventure seemed more remote all the time. His father was responsible for Grubber and Drum's being here. There was no doubt about it. No mistake. No coincidence. No kazoo, either. Sheesh.

Still, way back when, when the adventure had involved only the yellow stickers, hadn't his dad said the adventure was Rodney's? Hadn't he? Rodney would have to remind him.

"Ah," said Mr. Congruent. "I'm sure it was the *Vagabond Lover III*. Is that right?"

"I haven't any idea," said Grubber. Drum shook her head.

Mr. Congruent said, "Son, will you get the proper book of the encyclopedia?"

It's my adventure, Rodney wanted to shout. *You* should be getting books for *me*. But Rodney decided to be polite. At least until the matter of the space probe had been settled. It seemed only fair. Really.

Through gritted teeth, Rodney said, "Sure, Dad," and ran from the breakfast room. He beat on the hallway wall with his fist. He shook his head. He didn't know how much more of this he could stand.

When Rodney returned to the table, Grubber was

telling his parents about the House of Amazement, a place filled with mile after mile of unbelievable glittering exhibits. Still, to hear Grubber tell it, the House of Amazement was not so much a museum as it was a never-ending circus of alien thrills.

"Here's the book," Rodney said, and kind of dropped it in front of his father. It was a heavy book, a volume of the *Encyclopedia Cafeteria (A Feast for the Mind!).*

As he began to thumb through the book, Mr. Congruent said, "Something wrong, Rodney?"

You bet, Rodney shouted in his brain. Out loud, he said, "I hope not."

"Ah, here," said Mr. Congruent when he found the page. The article about the space program included a timeline with drawings of the various space probes and the year each was launched. His father pointed to the *Vagabond Lover III* and said, "Is that it?"

Grubber Young and Drum both looked at the book—not just at what was in the book, but at the book itself. "Quaint," Drum said, and Grubber nodded. At last Grubber looked at the picture that Mr. Congruent pointed to and said, "That's it, all right."

"Well, what do you know?" Mr. Congruent said, and sat back in his chair, obviously dumbfounded that anything had come of something for which he'd paid a quarter when he was just a kid.

Rodney, rubbing his hands together, said to his parents, "You guys must be pretty tired after your trip. I guess you'll be wanting to hit the old sackaroony while I help Grubber and Drum collect exhibits for the House of Amazement. Huh, Dad?"

Everyone looked at Rodney. He wondered if he appeared as desperate as he felt. But he wouldn't give up his kazoo playing for no reason. He couldn't. He stared at his dad, trying to read his expression. Mr. Congruent smiled this tentative little smile, as if he were thinking about something bittersweet and lost forever—maybe his exciting childhood, maybe the way Chocolatron tasted the first time he drank some. With his dad it was difficult to tell.

Mr. Congruent said, "Well, actually, that's right. Besides, your mother and I are pretty busy right now with this new Chocolatron advertising campaign."

"That's great, Dad," Rodney said with some relief. Almost immediately, his relief turned to suspicion.

Mr. Congruent said, "Now that that's settled, I suggest we do something about Grubber and Drum's appearance. They won't get half a block in the daylight."

Was his dad just being polite? Was this just a last gasp of helpfulness before his parents went to bed? Or was Rodney still being upstaged by a couple of adults who could not let go?

7

Monsters of Amazement

Grubber Young told them not to worry about what he and Drum looked like. "We figured out stuff like that long ago," he said.

Everyone except Rodney seemed entirely relaxed. Inside, he was a seething mass of frustration, and some of this feeling showed on the outside. He was stiff, and answered questions with short unenthusiastic statements. His parents looked at him a little strangely, but neither Grubber nor Drum seemed to notice.

When Grubber finished his Chocolatron, he went out to the *Ship of Amazement*. While he was gone, Drum explained her job. She said, "A finder looks for valuable vitamins, minerals, proteins, odds, ends, tchotchkies—whatever she's been hired to look for. She's a finder because she has a talent for finding things."

"You'll find a lot of interesting stuff here on Earth," Mr. Congruent said. He snapped his fingers. "I'll bet we could be a big help."

Drum grinned and said, "Great! Native guides! Wow!"

Wow, sure, thought Rodney without enthusiasm. Words welled up out of Rodney before he could stop them. "I thought this was *my* adventure." Rodney sounded angrier than he'd planned. But he was really too angry to care.

"It is," Mr. Congruent said. He looked a little bewildered.

"How can I have my own adventure with you guys around?" Rodney hated himself when he whined. The fact that he felt forced into it only made him angrier.

"Perhaps," said Mrs. Congruent, looking very much like a mom about to deliver a lecture, "we should discuss this in the kitchen."

"Will you excuse us?" Mr. Congruent said as the three of them got up.

When the kitchen door swung closed behind them, Mrs. Congruent said, "Now, Rodney."

Now, at the ultimate moment, Rodney was tongue-tied. He didn't enjoy being angry at his parents, and didn't really know how to approach his subject without making things worse. He could tell by the expressions on their faces that they were expecting to be offended in some way.

Finally, Rodney said, "I don't know what to say."

"What would Captain Conquer say?" Mr. Congruent said.

Following Captain Conquer's lead didn't appeal to Rodney. He didn't want anything to do with the captain. Besides, Captain Conquer's thoughts on the matter didn't seem relevant. Nobody'd ever tried to take an adventure away from *him*. He was a hero. Keeping himself under tight control, Rodney said, "It's about this adventure."

"A doozy, isn't it?" said Mr. Congruent.

"Well, yeah. It is."

"Then what's the problem?" Mrs. Congruent said.

"Well, it's this. I really appreciate you letting me open that envelope and wear the sticker and throw the glitter and all. And it really *is* a doozy of an adventure. But whose adventure is it?"

"Whose—?" Mr. Congruent said.

"—adventure is it?" Mrs. Congruent said.

"You know," Rodney said. "Is it yours or mine? I can't play the kazoo anymore. I ought to get something out of the deal."

"Why, it's yours, of course," Mr. Congruent said. He leaned against the sink and folded his arms.

"But you are the ones who fed Grubber and Drum Chocolatron, and you're the ones who will make the deal to sell it to the House of Amazement. And Dad is the one who suggested they needed disguises, and then offered to help them search for exhibits. And you don't look as if you're ever going to leave me

71

alone with them." Stop whining, Rodney ordered himself.

Mr. Congruent folded his arms the other way. Mrs. Congruent rested one hand on her husband's shoulder. She said, "Don't you want our help?"

No, Rodney thought. He said, "I need to see if I can do this myself. I may never have another chance."

"We're just trying to help," Mr. Congruent mumbled. "We have a lot of experience in this area."

"You didn't have experience when you had your adventures when you were kids, and you did okay. I want the same chance to prove myself."

Nobody said anything for a while. Beyond the door, Rodney heard Drum say something in a voice too soft to understand.

"Listen, Dad," Rodney said, "I know that this adventure is really yours because you're the one who sent the message on the *Vagabond Lover III*. If you want it back, you can have it. But if it's mine, well...." He shrugged. "You know." Did they know? Were they capable of understanding? Or were they, as unusual as they were, too adult?

Mr. Congruent looked at his wife. Mrs. Congruent looked back. They seemed to be having some kind of private conversation without words. At last Mr. Congruent said, "You're absolutely correct, Rodney. Your mother and I have been selfish. We've had our adventures. It's only right that you have yours. Our in-volvement would deprive you of the experience of your lifetime. Besides, you seem to have paid for it already."

"Really?" Rodney could not quite believe this was actually happening. He quivered with anticipation. The opportunity of a lifetime. It would make or break him. He felt the way he did before a big test.

"Sure," Mr. Congruent said, "We're going to bed. Long day. Right, Penny?"

"Of course."

"I love you guys," Rodney said. The three of them shuffled around, awkwardly trying to hug each other all at once.

A moment later Mr. and Mrs. Congruent were leaning into the breakfast room and wishing Drum good-night. "I'm sure that you and Rodney will manage just fine," Mrs. Congruent said, and sniffled.

A moment later they were gone, leaving Rodney to face two aliens from space with the knowlege that he was really on his own at last. He wished he had the confidence to match. It will come, he told himself. It will have to come.

Grubber Young came back pushing a contraption that looked like a circular framework held aloft at one side by a pole. The pole rose like a single leg from the apex of a V-shaped support that looked like a splayed foot. The three small wheels squeaked as he rolled the thing across the floor.

"This," Grubber said, "is the Shower Curtain of Deception." He looked around and said, "Where are your parents?"

Irritably, Rodney said, "They decided to go to bed."

"A little abruptly, I think," Grubber Young said. He continued staring at the door between the breakfast room and the kitchen. "I like them."

"Yes," said Drum. "I like their attitude toward the unexpected."

"You are so right," said Grubber. "You don't often find people who've dealt with the Puddentakers and lived to tell about it."

This entire situation was not going the way Rodney had expected it to. Angrily, Rodney said, "I'm here. My parents are not. Everything will be fine. Trust me. After all, I've been trusting you two."

Grubber Young seemed surprised by Rodney's outburst. He recovered and said, "Absolutely correct. We'll muddle through somehow."

Muddling wasn't what Rodney had in mind, but it was an improvement over whining. He said, "Sure. And we'd better get to it."

"You're right. I was just about to say that myself." Grubber waved his hands in the air like a magician and said, "I will now demonstrate the Shower Curtain of Deception."

He stepped under the circular framework, so that he stood in the opening between the feet. "Hey, presto!" he cried, and with a single motion he pulled a shower curtain around him on the framework. Rodney admired Grubber's showmanship.

Suddenly, Grubber Young was gone. In his place stood a large but normal-looking man dressed in a green plaid suit. A smoking cigar was stuck in his mouth, but there was no cigar smell. He looked pretty strange in that suit, but he was undeniably human.

"Grubber?" Rodney said.

"I'm still here," Grubber said in his familiar voice while the mouth of the man in the green suit moved. "But my image is distorted by the Shower Curtain of Deception."

"He can go anywhere like that," Rodney said.

"And notice the wonderful cigar," Drum said proudly. "No smell."

"No tar or nicotine, either." Grubber flicked an ash into the air. It evaporated before it hit the floor. "It's just an *image* of a cigar, after all. But it's the image of a very good cigar."

With a shiver, Rodney realized that Grubber might have made his first mistake. He'd admitted earlier that the Slignathi were masters of disguise, and here he was being pretty deceptive himself. Could Grubber be a Slignathi? And if he was, why would Drum still be searching for them? Unless Grubber had been deceiving her all along. But the Slignathi weren't real anyway, were they? Rodney had too many questions and nobody whose answers he could trust. He'd just have to stay alert. Rodney said, "What about Drum?"

Drum said, "I've never been able to use the Shower Curtain of Deception. It makes me itch." She made scratching motions under one arm.

"I'll bet some of my clothes would fit you," Rodney said. He took Drum upstairs, and they went through his closet and dresser together. While they did this, Rodney was aware of the longing he'd felt during the dream brought on by the yellow sticker. It was part of Drum's essence, Grubber Young had explained. Yet neither Grubber nor Drum had mentioned the longing in particular. On the contrary, Drum seemed happy with life, almost giddy, as if it constantly charmed and entertained her.

Hoping to learn more, Rodney said, "You must see a lot of neat stuff while you're knocking around the universe."

Drum had her fingers on a hanger holding a Hawaiian shirt. She looked at Rodney seriously for a long time. She said, "Neat stuff, yeah. But not always the right stuff."

"Right stuff?" Rodney said.

"You know. For the exhibits and all." Drum pushed the Hawaiian shirt aside and then just stared into the closet.

"Sure," Rodney said. "For the exhibits." Rodney could not help being jealous of somebody who got to hang around a great place like the House of Amazement, but Drum shook her head as if there were a lot of things Rodney didn't know. She held up a pair of jeans. "What about these?"

And yet nothing in the House of Amazement satisfied her. Drum was looking for that evil thing. Rodney said, "You must have a dream exhibit."

"Dream exhibit?"

"You know—something big and important that you haven't found yet."

Drum turned around suddenly and looked at Rodney the way she had when she'd caught him using the Chocolatron Hotline. Angrily, she said, "Look, Rodney, we all have our little secrets, okay?"

"I was just—"

"You were just curious, I know. Well, you go ahead and be curious. What about these pants?"

The pants were fine, but that didn't satisfy Rodney. There was more to Drum than he could see if she got all bristly about her ambitions. If he got Grubber alone, he'd have to ask.

It wasn't long before Drum had on a shirt with blue stripes and a pair of Rodney's old jeans. On her feet were white cotton sweat socks and ancient penny loafers, each with a real penny in it.

"How do I look?" Drum asked, twirling in front of the mirror and trying to see how she looked from the back.

Rodney said, "I guess you could be a human who has some terrible disease. Most people will ignore you." Drum seemed pleased.

They went back downstairs where Grubber Young, in his human form, smiled at Drum and said that she looked terrific. He rubbed his hands together and said, "It's time for a little collecting."

"Absolutely," Drum said, her old enthusiastic self again.

As they walked together toward the front door, the wheels of Grubber's Shower Curtain of Deception squeaked.

"Need some Three-in-One oil?" Rodney said.

"No way," Grubber said. "If the squeaks go, the deception goes."

As he opened the front door, Rodney and the others heard a loud crash at the back of the house. He cried, "Hey!" and led the way toward the sound. As they ran, a deep forbidding voice filled the house and shook its frame. It said in Mobambi, "You cannot resist me! I am invulnerable!"

The sound of adventure, Rodney thought. He could handle it. He reached the den and stopped, causing the others to pile up behind him. Something had smashed through the back door, leaving a jagged hole that let in the cool night air. Broken glass, plaster, and wood were all over the floor. The thing that made the jagged hole was standing in the center of the room, tiny motors whining as it turned its head up and back, surveying the scene.

The thing was a robot. Its chest gleamed and looked like the grill of an old automobile. Its arms and legs looked as if they were made from the same angles and I-beams that bridges were made of; at the end of each arm, instead of hands, it had a bulky cylinder with a pointed nose—a thing that could only be a weapon. Its eyes were glowing spirals that turned constantly, drawing you in. When it saw Grubber Young and Drum, chrome teeth gnashed.

Once again the mighty voice boomed through the house. It said, "I have you this time, you monsters of amazement!" Motors whining, the robot lumbered toward them firing a web of laser beams.

Behind him, Rodney heard his father say, "Give 'em what fer, son!"

His parents were back. Couldn't expect them to stay in bed when explosions were happening downstairs. Rodney felt a strong urge to ask them for help, but he fought it. Feeling like a fool—soon to be a dead fool—he dodged death beams as he stepped forward and cried in Mobambi, "Trespassers will be prosecuted, buddy. You're in big trouble now."

8

The LTP

"Hokey Slignathi! It's Grits," Drum cried as she danced this way and that to avoid the shafts of red light.

Grits' weapons made a strange yowling noise as the bright-red beams slashed across the den's flowered wallpaper.

"There is no escape!" Grits rumbled.

The danger put Rodney into a state of heightened awareness. Things were bigger and brighter and moved more slowly than normal. Sound was louder. Afraid but game, he said, "You didn't tell us a robot was after you." He and his parents backed out of the den as Grits advanced. "Go back to bed," Rodney cried.

"Don't worry, Rodney," Mr. Congruent cried back. "We're just observing." He and his wife were wide-eyed with excitement. They kept pointing things out to each other.

Grubber said as he and Drum followed, "That's not a robot. It's a battle suit. Grits is the guy inside."

"There is no escape!" Grits rumbled again.

By this time they had backed out all the way to the living room. Rodney was relieved to see Mr. and Mrs. Congruent sit down on the couch; they followed the battle as if it were a play and Rodney were acting the lead. One less thing for him to worry about.

"Uh," said Rodney, "you're right, Grits! We've trapped you at last!" He spoke loudly and confidently. His voice hardly shook at all.

The battle suit stopped. Laser blasts fizzled, popped, and disappeared. The head of the battle suit swiveled to glare at Rodney. "What do you mean?" it said.

"We have you now. You're coming with us."

"What language is the robot speaking?" Mr. Congruent asked.

"It's Mobambi," Rodney said without turning away from Grits.

"How very clever of you to learn it," Mrs. Congruent said.

There was no time to explain the stickers. Rodney just agreed and smiled politely.

"Quickly," cried Grubber Young. "While the battle suit is still confused. We must overload its sensors!"

"Right," said Rodney. As he ran from the room, he switched on the radio. He leaped up the stairs two at a time and rummaged in his room. Downstairs, the radio was blaring a rock 'n' roll song:

Love me like a chain saw!
Love me like a hammer!
Love me till I'm used up!
Make me cry and stammer!

Rodney recognized it—a big hit by Nose Grease. He grabbed the black pebbled kazoo case and ran back down.

When he got back to the living room, Grits' battle suit stood in its center looking from side to side. The battle suit raised one arm and tapped itself on the side of the head. *Klang-klang!* It took a step forward.

Rodney quickly took out his electronic kazoo and braced himself, ready for the awful sound he'd come to expect. He took a deep breath and began to play the "Robin Hood Overture" by Rooski-Pedruski. To his delight, the music sounded the way it had before the yellow sticker had changed it. Rodney loosened up and began to sway with the music. The moment he began to play, Drum stuck her fingers into her ears.

The battle suit wobbled and began to turn around. "Hey, wait!" cried Grits' voice, neither so assured nor as rumbling as it had been before. As a matter of fact, to Rodney it sounded a little shrill. The battle suit marched back the way it had come. "You're going the wrong way!" cried the voice. "Gol dern the gol-dern battle computer," the voice grumbled.

Rodney followed with his kazoo. He pursued the

battle suit out the opening it had made earlier and watched it climb a ramp into a ship standing on sled runners next to the *Ship of Amazement*.

The second ship had a very classy black-with-silver-trim paint job, but even so it looked like a hawk designed by a plumber. Great kettles and tanks were connected by pipes and hoses. Along one tank the word DAISY was printed in Mobambi.

The ramp folded into the hawk's chest and Rodney stopped playing. Drum came up beside him and said, "What is that thing, anyway?"

"It's an electronic kazoo, a musical instrument. It belonged to my mom's father."

She took it from Rodney and looked in both ends. She fiddled with the dials. "What an awful noise it makes."

"I like it," Rodney said. "At least I did till I put on the yellow sticker."

"Of course. Actually, the sticker was designed only to teach the wearer to read Mobambi in preparation for his or her arrival on the *Ship of Amazement*. The trouble you had with the kazoo is a side effect, I guess. I hope it didn't cause you any problem."

Rodney remembered how terrible he felt when he thought he would never again play the kazoo. "Not much," Rodney said. "The side effect seems to have worn off, anyway."

"Yeah," said Drum, "side effects do that. The learning is more or less permanent. You'll know Mobambi forever."

"Couldn't hurt, I suppose," Rodney said. He carried the kazoo as they returned to the living room. The radio was off, and when he entered the room, his parents gave him a standing ovation. He smiled proudly and made a little bow. All the time he wondered if he would be able to get his parents back to bed.

Grubber Young was sitting on the couch next to Rodney's parents mopping his forehead with a big handkerchief that matched his suit. He puffed madly on his cigar. Still no smell.

"Who are you?" Mrs. Congruent said.

"That's Grubber," Drum said, and laughed.

"Shower Curtain of Deception," Grubber said, and peeked out at them with his real face.

"I'll be doggoned," Mr. Congruent said. "How does it work?"

Rodney could see that they were getting off the track. Pointedly, he said, "More important, who is this Grits guy?"

His parents looked at Rodney, a little surprised, but they didn't object when Drum said, "Grits is an old geezer who's been chasing us all over the galaxy for years. He's a prospector."

"Sometimes they go a little crazy," Grubber Young said.

"Right. Comes from living and working alone so much. As I was saying, he's a prospector. No doubt he thinks that Earth is the LTP."

"What's that mean?" Rodney said.

"LTP? It's the Legendary Treasure Planet." As Drum explained in a low mysterious voice, she built imaginary things in the air with her hands. She said, "They say that the galumphus goes there to die, leaving behind a skeleton of pure dilithium. Interstellar arms dealers open their secret bank accounts there. Rare baseball cards grow on trees. The mountains are chocolate, and the rivers flow with lemonade. That's what they say." She dropped her hands.

Grubber got his breath back and now looked a little calmer. "There are those who spend their entire lives searching for it. Grits is one of them." Mrs. Congruent frowned when he flicked an ash from his cigar, but when it disappeared before it reached the upholstery, her eyes widened.

Drum said, "I guess he wanted to make sure we never challenged his claim."

"It's true," said Grubber. "Grits and his boss are not the type to share."

"How did he find you?" Rodney asked.

"Ah," Grubber said. He waggled a finger in the air

and spoke seriously, as if what he said were of great portent. "Aboard his ship, the *Daisy*, he has an entire bank of dowsers tuned to our very being."

"Being?" said Mr. Congruent.

"It's kind of complicated," Grubber said.

"Dowsers?" said Rodney. "Like dowsing rods?"

"Exactly," said Grubber. "Using his dowsers, Grits can find us anywhere eventually." Grubber frowned. "Anywhere," he repeated.

While Grubber continued to frown, Drum said, "I don't think a free pass to the House of Amazement is going to cover the damage to your house."

"Certainly not," Grubber said. He pulled a magnifying pen from a pocket. "Allow me to present you with one of these."

Mrs. Congruent took the pen and looked at it dubiously.

Mr. Congruent said, "It's a *lot* of damage."

"I'm sure—" Grubber began.

He was interrupted by Mrs. Congruent, who said, "Why, dear, I believe our homeowner's insurance covers attacks by aliens."

Mr. Congruent snapped his fingers and said, "You're right. It's about time we got some good out of that policy."

"That's all settled, then," Grubber Young said. "Take a couple of passes to the House of Amazement anyway, with my compliments."

While Rodney's parents studied the silver tickets, Rodney piped up and said, "Well, I guess that settles that, huh guys?"

Mr. Congruent said, "I was just going to offer to help Grubber and Drum get Grits off their backs."

Mrs. Congruent gave him a little kick in the ankle.

"On the other hand," Mr. Congruent continued, "it's been a long day and I'll probably be on the phone with the insurance company all day tomorrow." He and Mrs. Congruent stood up. He bowed at Grubber Young and said, "I leave you in the capable hands of our son."

"Great," said Drum.

"Hmmm," said Grubber.

Mr. and Mrs. Congruent went upstairs again and Rodney said, "Now, about those dowsers."

Drum said, "By the time we get close enough to the *Daisy* to reset the dowsers or destroy them or whatever, those same dowsers have told Grits we're coming. He's always ready for us."

"See the problem?" Grubber wiggled his eyebrows at Rodney.

"Well, then," said Rodney slowly, thinking the problem through as he spoke, "why don't *I* sneak up on the *Daisy* while you and Drum are off somewhere else?"

Drum cried, "That's great!"

Grubber Young blew smoke rings at the ceiling. They were really extraordinary smoke rings too, because they turned and changed color as they rose. He said, "It's a crazy idea, but it just might work."

9

A Big Hand for
the Seventh Dimension

Rodney led them to the breakfast-room table, where they sat down. Grubber Young whipped out a sheet of paper and a pencil. He touched the pencil to the paper, but did not write anything. He said, "The *Daisy* is a very old ship, welded together from the bow of an ancient Alturian freighter, the forekettle of a two-century-old Kalodian Mitochondria, an aftkettle of a Skinless Frank—long in need of an overhaul, I might add—and all powered by a Decatur 650 Hypergrunt engine. The Decatur 650 is peculiar in that—"

"Do we have time for the lecture?" Drum said.

Grubber shrugged. "Perhaps on another occasion," he said. "All right, Rodney, here's what the inside of the *Daisy* looks like." Grubber drew a line on the paper.

"Wow," cried Rodney. The pencil not only drew a line but a three-dimensional wall, complete with gauges and controls. "With that and the magnifier you two could barter for a lot of beads, trinkets, and tchotchkies."

"You think?" Grubber Young said.

"Grits," said Drum.

"Ah, yes." Grubber Young continued to draw the *Daisy*'s main control room until a small 3-D model of it stood on the paper.

Rivets were everywhere, holding things together. Scattered around the floor of the big room were circular tanks, each topped by a cap from which big pipes extended in various directions and poked out through the ceiling. The only control panel had big metal throttles.

Drum laughed and said, "Grits has always been a little short on style."

"Still," said Grubber, "we must not underestimate him. I'm sure Rodney's parents would not."

"Neither do I," said Rodney. How long would the ghosts of his parents haunt him? "Show me what to do with the dowsers."

Grubber showed him where the dowser bank was kept. Rodney was to open a small access hatch and turn several dials at random. That would reset the dowsers.

"Seems simple enough," Rodney said.

"To the untrained eye, perhaps." Drum waggled a finger at him. "But one wrong move and your hand will end up in the seventh dimension."

The shock of hearing Drum's casual statement made Rodney stiffen. Fear was almost a physical pressure inside him. Still, he might *not* lose his hand, and even if he did, he would have a swell story to tell if anybody asked about it. Maybe he could get a hook. "Okay," he said. "Anything else I should know?"

"That's it. Here," said Grubber as he folded up the diagram. The paper folded flat, as if the diagram had been drawn with a regular pencil.

Rodney took the paper and unfolded it again, and the diagram was just as three-dimensional as it had been before. He watched closely between the sheets to see where the model went when he folded the paper, but he could not see the trick. He noticed Grubber and Drum smiling at him, so he folded the paper a last time and put it into his pocket. "Pretty neat," he said. "How's it done?"

"I have no idea," Grubber said. "I just buy 'em. I don't build 'em."

Rodney sighed, "Okay, then. I'll get my kazoo, put it into its case, and we can get started."

"Kazoo?" Grubber said as Rodney rose.

"The thing I used to chase Grits away." He got the kazoo and let Grubber inspect it as Drum had earlier.

Grubber got very excited. He said, "I have an artifact just like this back at the Planetoid of Amazement, but I never knew what it was called." He had Rodney write down the word KAZOO in both English and Mobambi. Grubber said, "An electronic noisemaker like that kazoo has real possibilities." He gave Drum a knowing nod. "Look what it did to Grits."

Rodney smiled. He liked the idea of being the owner of an interstellar weapon.

The night was beautiful, if a little cool. They climbed aboard the *Ship of Amazement* and raised the stairway. Inside, Grubber went to the control panel to put the ship's computer through its security program. "We don't want to make this too easy for Grits, after all. And we also don't want him to really do us damage."

Rodney looked through a porthole at the *Daisy* and said, "Why doesn't Grits just blow you away as you sit here?"

"He'd never do that," Grubber said.

Drum laughed and said, "He doesn't blow us away for the same reason we didn't let you use your communications device to call your air force."

"I get it," said Rodney. "Blowing you away would attract attention."

"A *lot* of attention," Grubber Young said. He hummed as he adjusted his board, and paid no further attention to Drum and Rodney.

Drum opened the tool locker and withdrew a small

leather folder. Inside it was a pocket full of tiny precise instruments—little hooks and scrapers and grabbers, even mirrors of varying sizes on long slim handles—that looked like the kinds of tools a dentist might use. Drum demonstrated how to use them on the dowsers.

Rodney closed the small leather folder and found that there was just room for it in his kazoo case.

"All set," Rodney said.

As she ushered him toward the hatch, Drum confided in a low voice, "Just one more thing that Grubber forgot to mention. Once you get the access hatch open, after you reset the dials, it would be a good idea for you to play a little song on your kazoo in the direction of a narrow pipe you'll find just under them."

"What'll that do?"

"Randomize the combination even further. Even if Grits has the right numbers written down someplace, they won't do him any good, because after the kazoo blast the numbers will not mean the same thing to the machine as they meant before."

Rodney nodded. Feeling very heroic, he marched after Drum to the main hatch.

"Thanks for the help, Rodney."

Rodney shrugged. "Somebody has to do it. I'm the one Grits can't read with his dowsers."

Drum nodded and said, "You'd make a great spy."

"Sure. Me and James Bond."

"Who?"

"Er, a famous human spy."

"How could a spy be famous? Everybody would recognize him, and he couldn't do much spying."

"It's kind of hard to explain. Can we do this?"

Drum nodded and lowered the staircase. After taking a quick look around, Rodney descended into the night. He crouched behind a small lemon tree his father had planted the year before. The sprinkling of light that came through the leaves was good camouflage. Anybody would be stepping on him before they saw him.

Rodney settled down to watch the *Daisy*. Crickets chirped until a gust of wind came up and stopped them. The leaves of the lemon tree rattled and Rodney shivered. Then the wind went away and a few seconds later the crickets began chirping again.

Rodney waited a long time. Lights in his parents' bedroom went off. Far away, traffic hissed and grumbled. A car horn honked once.

While he waited, Rodney had time to think about his parents, and the thoughts made him angry. He hoped they'd stay in bed. If they didn't, he'd go a little crazy. Rodney smiled at his realization that sometimes people were difficult to get along with even when you liked them.

Something aboard the *Daisy* moved. It was the ramp, growing from the chest of the ship. It touched the ground, and seconds later the battle suit lumbered down it and across the grass to the *Ship of Amazement*. The battle suit did not knock. It just pulled down the stairway, making it creak loudly in protest, and ascended slowly.

Rodney ran across the grass to the *Daisy*. The ramp vibrated a little beneath his feet, but he was up it in no time. He leaped across the threshhold and stood for a moment waiting and listening. The ship made no sound.

After passing through a short hallway, he came to the control room. It was exactly as Grubber Young had drawn it. He moved quickly to the proper access hatch and opened it. Inside was a void so blank that Rodney's eyes could not focus on the blackness. The drawer that held the dials he wanted to adjust was just below the void. After taking a deep breath to steady himself, he went to work with the dental tools. He wondered what life might be like with one hand feeling around in the seventh dimension.

Rodney heard a noise and froze. The noise continued. It was a series of wet slaps against the metal floor, as if a seal the size of an elephant were approaching. He smelled the dead-mildew musk of the thing before he saw it. Rodney pulled the tools from the access hatch, stood up, and turned around.

A thing leaped into the doorway, filling it. The creature was a big gray blob wearing a military hat and uniform jacket. The jacket was covered with medals and braid, some of which seemed to be alive. The arms of the jacket were much too short for the long bony arms of the thing. Each skinny finger had a suction cup on its tip. The terrible smell rose from the creature in waves so thick, Rodney was convinced he could see them. In a loud raucous voice it said in Mobambi, "You are trespassing. Exterminate. Exterminate."

Caught! Trapped! He stood there quivering, wondering if the thing would swallow him whole or nip him to death. *Come on, Rodney, think. Think like Captain Conquer if you must, but do it!* The thing was already menacing Rodney with its waving fingers. Trying not to allow his voice to shake, Rodney said the first thing that came into his mind. "You got a little problem here in your lock-up converter, bub." He pointed casually at the access hatch with a dental tool.

"Exterminate," the thing said, but with a little less certainty.

A plan came to Rodney. "Yeah," he said, "you need an entire new glombus. It'll take three weeks to get the part."

The thing roared and leaped at him, arms outspread. Rodney stepped to the side and one of the creature's hands touched the void inside the access hatch. The thing bellowed, and faster than Rodney could follow, it was drawn down to a point and sucked into the hatch.

"The seventh dimension," Rodney said in awe. The void remained as blank as it had been before.

He took a moment to get his breath and allow his heart to slow to normal, then he worked as fast as he could without making mistakes. He touched a flange with a hook and slowly pulled open the drawer. Nothing happened. Rodney sighed. Inside the drawer were four lighted dials. Each one had numbers in Mobambi around its edge. Below the dials was a narrow brown pipe that could have been made of copper.

He spun the first dial one way and then the other. It clicked as each number passed the top. Then he did the same thing with the other dials. He'd randomized them for sure.

He took his kazoo from his case and began to play scales as loudly as he could. He'd always hated practicing his exercises, and he figured that in this case, the fact that the song was boring might help. The copper pipe didn't seem to change, and Rodney wanted to give it a second chorus of scales, but he was afraid Grits might have left another creature around. Rodney had been here too long already.

He closed the access hatch and put away his kazoo and his tools. He walked back to the main hatch and looked for a pressure plate in the floor that he'd leaped over when he came in. Grinning with anticipation, Rodney jumped onto it with both feet. Immediately, a police siren whooped over and over again at the same time a loud electric bell began to ring.

Rodney leaped down the ramp and hid behind the lemon tree again. Seconds later the battle suit—presumably with Grits inside—wobbled down the stairs of the *Ship of Amazement*. It waddled quickly across the grass between the ships, looking as if it might topple over at any moment. It went up the ramp, and the ramp slid back into the ship after it. Rodney ran to the *Ship of Amazement*. By the time he got inside and looked out the porthole, he could see that they were high in the air and rising quickly.

A bright light lifted off from a dark patch on the ground and grew larger.

"Here comes Grits," Drum said.

"Hang on tight," said Grubber as he grasped the controls.

10

The Old Evasive Action

No matter how the scene outside the porthole tilted and turned, the couch was as steady as the one at home in his living room. Even so, Rodney became a little dizzy, and he felt better when he set his hand on the armrest.

Drum looked into a viewer that cast blue shadows up onto her face. "He's right behind us," she said delightedly.

Grubber said, "His dowsers are gone, so he must be eyeballing it."

"Clouds?" Rodney asked.

"Exactly," Grubber nodded.

He played the control panel as if it were a musical instrument and Rodney heard the engines work harder as the *Ship of Amazement* climbed.

"Still with us," Drum said.

The sky was usually overcast above Rodney's town, with either high clouds or smog—sometimes both. If on any given evening you could see a couple of the brighter stars, you were doing pretty well. Therefore, Grubber had no trouble finding a cloud bank. He plunged into it, and the ship was suddenly surrounded by a very pale silvery light.

Drum said, "Dowsers indicate he's right behind us."

"Heh heh," Grubber said. "We'll give him a little of the old evasive action."

From inside the cloud Rodney could see no landmarks, no airmarks—if there were such things—nothing at all to show that the ship was even moving. Yet both Grubber and Drum wore grim smiles on their faces.

"He's continuing in a straight line, following our old course," said Drum. She giggled.

"He won't see us when he breaks through the other side. Without his dowsers he won't know if we're waiting in the cloud bank, diving back toward Earth, or zooming around to the other side of the planet. Good work, Rodney."

"Thanks. But you don't know the half of it." He told them about the terrible creature he'd outsmarted aboard the *Daisy*.

"Probably a robot that was part of the security system," Grubber said as if he knew. He and Drum listened eagerly, and even as Rodney continued his story, he noticed they looked on him with new respect.

Grubber said, "That's pretty good, kid. Ever consider working in outer space?"

Rodney was surprised and excited by the question.

Certainly Grubber would not have asked it if he were still thinking about Rodney's parents. Rodney liked the idea too, though, in fact, he had *not* ever considered it. He said, "I'll need a summer job."

"My boy," Grubber said, "search no further."

Drum patted Rodney on the back, and they all hooked fingers.

Rodney said, "What will happen to Grits?"

Drum said, "Oh, if he doesn't find us and blow us away, he'll head back to Hutzenklutz Station."

"And be waiting for you two when you get there."

"Maybe," Drum said. "The *Daisy* is not very fast, as starships go."

"It's that old Decatur 650 Hypergrunt engine." Grubber rubbed his hands together and said, "But enough about Grits. I'm hungry enough to eat a Slignathi. That cup of Chocolatron happened a long time ago."

Rodney realized Grubber Young was right. He had had a long, trying day in school, and no dinner. A little nosh before turning in sounded like a good idea.

As far as Rodney could tell, the adventure was about over. They'd eat and he'd go home and his parents would want to hear everything. Tomorrow he'd probably have to go to school. His life would be back to normal, including his ability to play the kazoo, thank goodness. But for tonight, he liked to think that if he hadn't been there, the situation would have turned out differently. Their victory called for a special meal. Rodney said, "Let's eat at the *Cosmic Ray Diner*."

"What's that?" Drum said.

"It's a great place out at the edge of town. Rocky Smith designed and built it himself. He started with what was left of the full-size replica of the original ship from the *Rocky Smith, Space Commando* show and sort of remodeled it."

"Original ship?" said Drum. It was not an idle question. She looked a lot more interested than Rodney thought the conversation warranted. But maybe she was just an old TV buff like his parents. They knew everything there was to know about Rocky Smith, and over the years they'd force-fed most of it to him during dinner.

"Absolutely original," said Rodney. "The sponsor of the Rocky Smith show, Grain Zippys, had a contest whose first prize was a full-size replica of the *Cosmic Ray*, complete with bunk beds and a little kitchen and a control panel that lit up and made noise. My mom entered twenty-seven times."

"They must have sold a ton of Grain Zippys," Grubber Young said in awe.

Drum said, "Do you know who built her?" The casual tone in her voice was not altogether natural.

Rodney wondered what was going on. "Built her?"

he said. "The *Cosmic Ray?* My parents never said, but Rocky Smith might know. Anyway, years later, Rocky Smith himself found the full-size replica of the *Cosmic Ray* in some empty lot. He brought it home, fixed it up, and turned it into a diner."

Grubber Young said, "It sounds as if the *Cosmic Ray* would make a great exhibit."

Rodney looked at Grubber with suspicion and said, "You'd have to talk to Rocky about that."

"Don't worry about a thing," said Grubber. "I was just thinking out loud. Let's eat."

Drum cried, "Yeah! Let's eat! Food! Give me eat!" She giggled in a loose and crazy way.

Drum had always seemed a little excitable, but now she seemed to have lost control of her emotions entirely. Unless she was *really* hungry and she *really* wanted to try Earth food, something else was also going on. While watching her, Rodney said to Grubber, "If you fly close enough to the ground for me to see the streets, I can probably guide us there."

"Hey! What an idea." Drum grabbed the controls from Grubber and adjusted them.

"You must be even hungrier than I am," Grubber said, and laughed. He turned to look at Rodney, and seriousness fell over his face like a mask. Rodney shrugged. He certainly didn't know why Drum was acting so strange. Grubber looked back at Drum and laughed again.

The front-loading porthole of the *Ship of Amazement* tilted toward the ground, and Rodney saw the city spread out like a big black map with light shining up through tiny holes along the streets. Rodney got his bearings from a housing project that was laid out in the shape of diamonds, and told Drum which way to go.

As they flew along, Drum chuckled and said, "What a doofus that Grits is."

"Doofus?" Rodney said. "He almost killed all of us."

"Drum may be understating the case just a little. But the fact is, Rodney, that Mara, the lady Grits works for, and I have been competitors for a long time. Our rivalry has become kind of a game. I win a little. She wins a little. Neither of us really wants to hurt the other very much, or the game is over."

"He looked pretty eager to me," Rodney said.

"True, true," Grubber said. "Not even Mara can control Grits all the times, though she has better luck than most." He winked at Rodney. "I think he's kind of sweet on her." The thought seemed to please him.

Drum said, "Doofus," and laughed.

Not just a screw loose, thought Rodney. Maybe an entire transmission. Out loud, he said, "I guess that when Grits gets home, he'll just reset his dowsers and everything will be back the way it was."

"If he can figure out how," said Drum.

"There it is," Rodney cried.

The *Cosmic Ray Diner* stood at the border between a brightly lit parking lot and a huge oblong of darkness—an open field. From the air the diner looked like a ballpoint pen lying on a table. A red light at the tip of its nose blinked on and off.

The mighty engines of the *Ship of Amazement* roared as it dropped ever lower over the open field, then faded to nothing as the ship touched the ground with the familiar bump.

"I need a cheeseburger and an order of fries," Rodney said.

Drum nodded. "It sounds good to me," she said.

They were about to leave the *Ship of Amazement* when Drum said, "Aren't you going to take your kazoo?"

"Why?" Rodney asked. "Won't it be safe here?"

"Sure," Drum said. "Plenty safe. Safe as gravity." She laughed. She was doing a lot of laughing lately. She laughed again and walked out the hatch.

Should Rodney take the advice of an alien from space who had suddenly snapped? Probably. His father had said that part of an adventure was expecting the unexpected. This situation seemed to qualify.

Rodney went back to get his black pebbled case off the couch, then hurried to meet Grubber Young on the dark field. Drum was already marching toward the light. As he and Grubber marched behind her across the rough ground, the wheels of the Shower Curtain of Deception squealed. They were approaching the diner from the back. The light from the cars and the parking lot and the city on the other side gave it a halo.

"Well, I'll be a Slignathi's uncle," said Grubber. "The *Cosmic Ray Diner* looks like the latest model Starship Club emergency ship!"

"Yeah," said Drum. "What do you know?" She did not act very surprised. Grubber seemed as confused about Drum as Rodney was.

Then Grubber himself got distracted by the *Cosmic Ray*. He said, "I'm sure it's their new Galahad series. See those fins?"

"You recognize the diner?" said Rodney, astonished.

"Of course," said Grubber. "I'm a member of the Starship Club, so every month I get a copy of the Starship Club magazine. It contains interesting articles on interstellar safety regulations, new club services, and descriptions of the latest emergency vehicles."

"Tell me about the emergency vehicles."

"Well, suppose you crash-landed on a planet and had no way to get home. If you had a Starship Club membership card, you could get home in one of their ships. It's all part of the service."

"And the *Cosmic Ray Diner* looks like one of those

Starship Club ships?"

"Could actually *be* one. They're everywhere."

"But how would it have gotten to Earth?"

By this time they'd come to the edge of the dark field. On the other side of the *Cosmic Ray Diner* Rodney heard the sound of traffic and of people slamming car doors and of laughter. A delicious greasy smell weighed down the air. That cheeseburger and fries sounded better than ever. Grubber said, "Maybe it never got to Earth."

"Huh?"

"It was built right here." Seeing Rodney was still confused, Grubber Young turned to him and said, "Look, kid: There are a lot of things about the universe you don't know right now. One of the things is that beings from other worlds can influence you Earthpeople in subtle ways you never even suspected. The Starship Club beings must have influenced the Earthpeople who built that ship so it would turn out this way."

Rodney did not like the sound of that. "What about wars and stuff?"

"What about them?"

Rodney decided that knowing how much aliens could influence Earthpeople might be more important than knowing about two geeks from space who wanted to take home burger wrappers. He hoped that when he had another chance to call the Chocolatron Hotline somebody would believe him.

Sounding more like Drum than he wanted to, Rodney laughed and said, "I saw it in a movie once. Not a very good movie, I guess."

"What happened?"

Rodney chuckled again. Maybe if they thought he was a doofus, they wouldn't suck out his brain. "Well, in this movie, wars and prejudice and poverty here on Earth are caused by alien beings who want to upset things so they can have the Earth for themselves— because it's the Legendary Treasure Planet, for instance."

Drum was staring fixedly at the *Cosmic Ray*. Rodney didn't even know if she'd been listening to their discussion.

Grubber said, "Hey, that's actually pretty good. But I don't think it's possible. I don't know any alien species that can influence events on *that* scale. Certainly I don't know of any who can change one being's basic feeling about another." He shook his head. "If terrible things like that happen on Earth, my guess is that Earthpeople are behind it."

So they didn't need to suck out his brain after all. Rodney didn't know if he was comforted by Grubber's explanation. Was it better that humans were nasty on their own hook, or that they were forced into being nasty by aliens?

Hoping to change the subject, Rodney said, "Here on Earth, we have an organization like the Starship Club."

"I thought you people didn't have starships," Grubber said.

Drum walked to the end of the *Cosmic Ray*, where she stopped and leaned around the jet. She seemed to be vibrating to music inside her head. Rodney leaned around her and saw the well-lit parking lot busy with cars. Grubber came up next to him.

"Not for starships," Rodney said, "for automobiles."

"I see." Grubber smiled. "I guess that would work. Does your club supply special emergency automobiles around the world so that if your car breaks down, you can use one of theirs?"

"Well, no."

"Not really a full-service club, I guess." He inhaled deeply. "What is that wonderful smell?"

"Grease," said Rodney and smacked his lips. "It's not good for anybody, but most people eat it anyway."

"I thought we were going to have cheeseburgers," said Drum.

"Same thing," Rodney said.

11

The Ultimate
Cosmic Ray Experience

The words COSMIC RAY DINER were painted on the side of the building in sharp letters that looked like lightning bolts. As they walked down its length to the main entrance at the other end, Grubber Young couldn't take his eyes off the parking lot. He exclaimed, "Look at the fins on that baby!" And "Chrome! I love chrome!" and "Great Slignathi! A two-tone, four-barrel ragtop!"

After his last comment, Grubber ran over to the guy who was just getting out of the car. Rodney watched with shocked surprise. He would have stopped Grubber, but he was fascinated by the exchange going on.

Grubber held out a magnifier pen, but the guy shook his head. Grubber added a three-dimensional pencil, but the guy only laughed and walked toward the diner, shaking his head. When Grubber returned to where Rodney was waiting, his enthusiasm was undiminished. "This is incredible. I need an automobile exhibit back at the Planetoid of Amazement. I don't know how I got along without one. What do you say, Drum? Where's Drum?"

Rodney said, "She went inside. What's wrong with her, anyway? She acts the way my father acts when he drinks coffee instead of Chocolatron."

"Maybe she's just up for a cheeseburger," Grubber said, as if he didn't believe it himself. He and Rodney climbed the metal stairway under the striped awning.

A long counter ran the length of the diner, and booths lined the walls. The air was warm and steamy and full of good smells—hot dogs and burgers and chili and day-old doughnuts and chocolate syrup all mixed together—but for some reason, it wasn't a disgusting smell; it was great. Every time he came here, Rodney was reminded again how much he liked this place. There were no menus, just chalkboards on the wall behind the counter. Everybody seemed to be talking and laughing and having a good time. A guy in a white T-shirt, pants, and paper hat ran up and back behind the counter taking orders.

Grubber stood at the door, nodding and smiling. Just about everybody did that the first time they came here. Even Drum was doing it. "Shall we sit?" Grubber said.

"To get the ultimate *Cosmic Ray* experience, you must sit at the counter," Rodney said.

"I wouldn't have it any other way," Grubber said, and he went to sit down. Drum sat down next to him, and Rodney sat down next to her. She was looking around as if the *Cosmic Ray Diner* were the most fascinating place in the world.

The man in white came over. He was a big guy who'd gone to fat a little, but he had wide heroic shoulders and a jutting chin. Blue piercing eyes looked at them, and his voice rumbled, "What'll you have?"

"Hi there, Rocky," Rodney said.

"Is that you, Rodney?"

"I was in here only last week."

"Right. Right. How're your mom and dad?"

"They're fine. These are my friends, Grubber Young and Drum. This is Rocky Smith, formerly Rocky Smith, Space Commando, now owner and operator of the *Cosmic Ray Diner*."

"Delighted to meet you," Grubber said, and shook his hand. "Space Commando, eh? I guess you know what a great ship the Starship Club Galahad model is."

"Huh?"

Quickly, Rodney said, "He's talking about your old TV show. Aren't you, Grubber?"

"Sure. Of course." Grubber waved his hands in the air.

"You'll have to put away that cigar, Mr. Young. You're in the no-smoking section."

Grubber shrugged and stuck the imaginary cigar behind his ear.

"What'll you have?"

They ordered cheeseburgers, fries, and chocolate shakes all around. While they waited for the cook to make up their order, a crowd of people who all seemed to know each other finished their food and left, leaving the diner much quieter. Carrying empty plates, Rocky walked past them and said, "Maybe now we'll have a chance to talk, eh, Rodney?"

"Sure, Rocky."

Rocky Smith brought their food, and went to wait on another table. Grubber and Drum looked with curiosity at what Rocky Smith had placed before them. Grubber poked his cheeseburger with one finger. Drum sniffed her chocolate shake.

"It's okay," said Rodney. "Trust me." He took a big juicy bite of his cheeseburger. It was delicious, exactly what he needed here at the ragged end of a very long, exciting night.

Grubber and Drum began to take small bites and small sips. But as they ate they built momentum, and soon they were scarfing down the food with the same enthusiasm as Rodney.

Rocky Smith took up a position a little ways down the counter, wiping it in big circles with a white towel. "You guys like to eat?"

"Eat what?" Grubber said.

"Yeah, I like to eat," Rodney said. It was an old joke between them.

Rocky Smith chuckled. "So, Rodney, what's new?"

"We got some advertising in the mail for Rocky Smith signature luggage."

Rocky shook his head. "Those guys at Norby's You Break It—You Bought It Novelty Company are going to make a fortune."

"Not you?"

"No way. Back when I signed my contract with Harv Fishbein Productions, who knew that luggage rights would be important?"

"Yeah. Who knew?" Rodney casually swished a french fry in a pool of catsup. Grubber Young watched him carefully and began to do the same thing.

Drum said, "So, tell me about the *Cosmic Ray*." She smiled at him around her straw.

Grubber's eyebrows went up. He stared at Drum in horror. Rodney wondered if Drum were crazy enough to announce she was from outer space.

Rocky Smith pulled in a straw wrapper with his towel and moved closer to them. "I didn't really have much to do with it at first. Some guy in the Harv Fishbein Productions art department designed it, I guess."

"And they built it out of the usual stuff?" Rodney said, hoping that if he couldn't change the subject, he could deflect it a little.

"Sure. Plywood and cardboard and old army surplus equipment. Considering the budget, they did pretty good."

Rodney glanced at Grubber and went on, "Not metal or anything you could take into space?"

"Naw," said Rocky. "Why? That would be too expensive. Besides, the thing was just going sit on a soundstage all day. The prize replica was built from the same stuff—it was never really going into space either."

That was all Rodney wanted to know. The prize *Cosmic Ray* was a prop, just like the set where they did the show. If some alien from the Starship Club had manipulated an Earthperson into designing and building it, he'd done a pretty poor job. Rodney glanced at Grubber Young, who was placidly dipping fries into catsup one at a time and eating them. Drum seemed entranced by Rocky Smith's story.

Rocky Smith stopped moving his towel and stared into the air as if he were looking back in time. "Some guy named Doug Bowser won the full-size replica of the *Cosmic Ray* in the Grain Zippys contest. Every kid in America was jealous of him the day they delivered it on a flatbed truck. Years later, when I wanted to open a diner, I tracked down Mr. Bowser. He told me that when he was a kid he'd moved and his parents had forced him to sell the *Cosmic Ray* to a carnival. He had no idea what happened to it after that."

"What did you do?" Drum said around a mouthful of fries.

"I spent the next few years tracking it down. I found it at last in a weedy field outside Edmond, Oklahoma. The carnival had abandoned it there. It was pretty beat-up."

Drum said, "How beat-up, exactly?"

"Oh, the paint was peeling, a lot of the army surplus equipment was gone, but the hull was still in pretty good shape."

Drum nodded with apparent relief.

"Anyway," said Rocky Smith, "I spent a lot of time and money converting it into a diner, but I'm not sorry." He looked around proudly.

Rocky Smith slapped the counter and said, "Just once, though, I'd like to have a *real* space adventure. With real spaceships and real aliens. Without worrying about the rotten budget." Rocky Smith kept shaking his head as if he couldn't believe his bad fortune, never having had a real space adventure.

Rodney sympathized, and almost told him that a couple of real aliens were sitting across the counter, but it wasn't Rodney's secret to tell. He was about to suggest that Grubber and Drum give Rocky Smith a break and tell him the truth when a voice called out, "Grubber!" It was a silly voice, as if the speaker were talking through his nose.

Everybody in the place turned to look at the new arrival. It was a small creature; the top of its head barely cleared the tabletop. He—it may have been an it for all Rodney knew—had big almond shaped eyes, no ears, and a pair of slits for a nose. He had no teeth, but the sharp-lipped mouth of a turtle. Even in the well-lit diner, his skin glowed with a pleasant golden light. At the moment he was wearing a leather vest, a pair of worn boots that came nearly to his knees, and a triangle of big red bandanna that hung from his neck. On his head was a beat-up old cowboy hat with the front brim bent up against the crown. He was also wearing what looked like a scuba diver's mask.

He raised what was certainly a weapon and aimed it in Grubber Young's direction. Which was also, in a manner of speaking, Rodney's direction. Apparently, adventure would continue. Rodney only hoped that he would live long enough to enjoy it.

"Grits," Grubber Young and Drum said together, both shocked.

12

Captive Audience of
the Starship Club

Even as Grubber and Drum spoke, other customers, willing themselves to be invisible, slid toward the door. Grits stepped forward, allowing them to escape. He obviously had no interest in them. Soon, the only people left in the diner with Grits were Rodney, Grubber Young, Drum, and Rocky Smith. Even the cook had gone.

"I guess you thought you were pretty foxy, didn't you?" Grits said.

"What's he saying?" Rocky Smith said. "I can't understand a word of it."

Rodney suddenly realized that Grits was speaking Mobambi. Rodney said, "This is Grits, Rocky—the real alien you've been waiting for."

"A bad guy, huh?" Rocky said.

"A regular Slignathi of a guy," Grubber said.

Shocked, Grits asked, "What's that about Slignathi?"

"Just a figure of speech," Grubber said. Then he

burst out, "We're astonished to see you, Grits."

"I'll bet you are, after all I've been through."

"Been through?"

"I never expected you to try blowing me up with my ship."

"Blowing you up?" Grubber was genuinely surprised. He was so surprised that he said, "All we did was randomize your dowsers."

"Hah. Is that what you call it when you block up somebody's fuel line, and that same somebody has to bail out, barely escaping with his life?"

"Barely?" Grubber said. "But we didn't—Rodney, what did you do to Grits' ship?"

"Just what you and Drum told me to do."

"You varmint!" Grits cried. "Having *Earthpeople* do your dirty work for you." He said "Earthpeople" as if he were swearing.

Grubber, still trying to make sense of the situation, said, "How did you find us?"

Grits whooped and threw his hat on the floor and picked it up and plunged it onto his head. "I'm a member of the Starship Club, ain't I? I can home in on the nearest Starship Club emergency ship, can't I? This here's a Starship Club emergency ship, ain't it?"

"Dumb luck," Grubber said. "What happened to the *Daisy?*"

"I told you! It blew up! I got out just in time! And

now I'm going to blow up the three of you!" He raised his weapon again.

Rodney realized this was a desperate situation. Heroic stuff needed to be done. Even as Grits' arm rose, Rodney threw the remains of his chocolate shake at Grits' mask. Grits howled and took a wild shot. Fireworks hit a coffee urn, causing it to explode into blue and silver sparkles.

As a glob of chocolate ice cream dripped brown legs in front of Grits' eyes, Rocky Smith leaped over the counter, grabbed Grits by the wrist of his shooting arm, and twisted it behind his back. Then he hustled Grits out the main entrance.

"I think Grits just made Rocky's day," Rodney said.

Grubber stood up and said, "You'd better go, Rodney. We'll want to leave before Grits comes back."

"No way. I'm going with you." It hadn't occurred to him that this was a possibility till he said it.

Grubber and Drum shared a glance. "It's a long way across that open field," Drum said. "He'd be a terrific target."

"All right," said Grubber. "We don't have time to argue. Drum?"

From her kangaroo pocket, Drum had already taken out a blue card. It was flashing and beeping. From somewhere in the diner came an answering beep. Drum followed the sound to the window between the kitchen and the rest of the diner. She matched the card like a puzzle piece into a flashing place where the tile directly below the window was missing. Once the card was in place, she slammed shut the window and a lot of things happened at once.

With a growl of machinery the main entrance closed, while the square windows that looked out onto the parking lot irised down into portholes. The remaining coffee urn opened like a flower, opened again and opened *again* until it opened onto nothing. The stools along the counter grew at odd angles until their cushions braced against the ceiling. The booth at the front of the diner turned to face the front port, while other booths tilted to reveal control consoles on what had been their undersides. The counter rose slowly, revealing blinking lights along the sides.

When the furniture stopped moving, a creature appeared in the space that had been inside the coffee urn. More than anything, it looked like a pile of blue strips of carpeting tacked together at the top. In Mobambi it said calmly, "Welcome to your Starship Club emergency vehicle. Please prepare for blast-off."

The three of them hurriedly got into the acceleration couches—what had formerly been the booth at the front of the diner. Seconds later, a roar jarred Rodney's bones, and the *Cosmic Ray Diner* leaped into the sky.

The clouds were gone. The sky outside the front port was the most beautiful and the most frightening thing Rodney had ever seen, making it difficult for him to catch his breath. The ship was floating in a huge empty blackness that went on forever, cold and hard and sprinkled with bright points. At the tip of the ship's needle nose the red light blinked casually in astonishing contrast to the blackness around it.

Until the diner actually began to change, Rodney hadn't believed all that stuff about the *Cosmic Ray* being a Starship Club emergency ship. If it hadn't been for a faint rumble and a slight vibration, the diner might still have been attached to the ground even now.

With some effort, he looked away from the port and back into the diner to catch anything else that might convert into another bank of computers or a ray gun or something. Though he was probably safe enough at the moment, Rodney was not confident about his future. He'd wanted to go with Grubber and Drum, and here he was, but he had no idea what to do next, no idea what might be required of him. Even the present moment was full of mysteries.

He said, "What I don't understand is how a prop ship made out of plywood can fly in space at all."

"What prop ship?" Grubber Young said.

"This prop ship. The *Cosmic Ray.*"

With some delight, Drum said, "The *Cosmic Ray* isn't a prop. It's built from all kinds of power crystals and rare metals and high-grade plastics. If an alien can manipulate humans into building the ship in the first place, is it so difficult to believe they can manipulate humans into believing they are building the ship out of plywood and surplus military parts?"

"Well, yeah. For one thing, what about the budget? Even if the guy who built the ship looked at metal sheeting and saw plywood, the guy who paid the bills would notice the difference. Or the guy who got paid would. *Somebody* would."

Grubber laughed and said, "You Earthpeople think you know everything. The fact is that Harv Fishbein paid only what he expected to pay for a prop ship. The rest of the tab was subtly picked up by the Starship Club."

Rodney rested his hand on the control console. They were here on this ship in space, its blinking red nose pointing proudly at the stars. There was no denying that. He said, "But the aliens aren't responsible for wars and poverty?"

"No way," Grubber said with finality. "I'm going to

look around." He stood up and moved back toward what had been the kitchen.

Drum seemed content to just sit on her acceleration couch watching the stars with a half smile on her face. Rodney sat opposite her trying to puzzle things out while Grubber made puttering noises. Maybe he should just accept what seemed to be true and work with it. If something else turned out to be true, he would work with that. Rodney's head swirled with convertible diners and aliens who could fool Earthpeople. Amazing. And then there was Drum. Something odd was going on that even Grubber didn't know about.

Rodney was concentrating so hard he jumped when the blue-carpet creature from the coffee urn said, "Welcome again to the Starship Club's latest emergency ship, part of the Galahad series. You are now on your way to the destination programmed into your membership card. No further action on your part is necessary. We hope you enjoy the ride." The image of the creature wavered for a second. It began to speak again. "It will be six standard days before you arrive at"—the image wavered again—"Hutzenklutz Station,"—it wavered again—"and during that time I would like to tell you about our other Starship Club services and travel opportunities." The creature disappeared and was replaced by a thing that looked like a fire hydrant waving thin hoselike cartoon arms at a thing that looked like one of those old-fashioned penny gum-ball dispensers, the kind with the gum inside a glass globe. The voice of the carpet creature said, "No matter where you're going, the Starship Club can help you have a better time."

"Is that thing going to advertise at us for six standard days?" Rodney said.

"Probably," said Drum. "Hey," she went on, "it's a small price to pay for getting home in one piece."

"Can we shut it off?"

"If I know the Starship Club," said Drum, "probably not."

Drum stood up and looked around, satisfied by what she saw. Rodney said, "What about Rocky Smith? If you think about it, this is his ship."

Drum said, "Maybe he has insurance too."

"Maybe," said Rodney. "For a couple of guys who came to Earth just to say hello, you've done a lot of property damage. And here you are stealing some guy's diner."

"Don't worry about it, Rodney," Drum said a little hotly. "My, er—our need is greater than his. We'll make everything up to Rocky Smith, and to your parents too. Eventually. Somehow." She stared out the front port and shook her head. "But I don't know when we'll be able to take you home."

"At the moment, I'm perfectly happy here. Trust me."

"Hey," Grubber called from the engine room, which had formerly been the kitchen, "this means you'll get a chance to see what Hutzenklutz Station hospitality is all about."

"I'm looking foward to it." Rodney yawned and said, "If you're not expecting any more excitement, I could use a few hours of sleep." Rodney made sure his kazoo was safe beneath his own acceleration couch, then lay down and willed his body to relax.

Rodney found the blinking of the nose light hypnotic. He fell asleep watching it while he tried to get used to the fact that his real adventure had started at last. He was aboard a diner going to the Planetoid of Amazement. That seemed pretty straightforward, at least. But what about Drum? Why had she begun to act weird all of a sudden? He'd have to discuss the situation with Grubber Young. Evidently, they'd have plenty of time.

The last thing he remembered hearing was the friendly thrum of the ship's engines and the cadences of the blue-carpet creature telling him what a good deal it was to be a member of the Starship Club.

Rodney awoke to see a bear leaning over the control console. Not yet fully awake, he leaped from his acceleration couch and stood there breathing hard. Back where the coffee urn used to be, the blue-carpet creature was going on about tour-guide service to a place called Trochenbrod. The bear turned around and in a pleasant growling voice it said, "Glad to see you're awake, Rodney. Take a look at this."

Of course, the bear was just Grubber in his natural form. Once more he wore only the stool helmet and his utility belt. At the moment he was pointing at the viewscreen above the control console.

Still feeling a little silly about not recognizing Grubber, Rodney looked at the viewscreen. Most of the screen held zillions of cubic miles of space. But in the center of it was a glowing white square.

"What is it?"

Grubber said, "The *Ship of Amazement*."

"Who's aboard?" Rodney said with surprise.

"Listen," said Grubber, and touched a switch. Grits' angry voice blasted into the room: "—and then I'm going to unravel your molecules like a sweater and squirt them into a black hole where they'll burn forever until they come out the other side in a white hole and I can assemble you again in the form of a bucket of slime that I can pour all over the Vile Upchuck Beast of Bertha, and then I'll really get tough. I'll dismemberize—" Grubber touched the switch again and Grits' voice stopped. Grubber said, "He's been going on like that for hours."

"He doesn't have my parents with him, does he?"

"I don't think so. Why would he?"

"No special reason," Rodney said. "What are we going to do?"

"Nothing. We'll beat him to Hutzenklutz Station by a standard day or two. Plenty of time to get ready."

"The transponder?" Drum asked.

Grubber and Rodney looked at her over their shoulders. Drum appeared the way she had when Rodney first saw her, like an intelligent Kangaroo. In one hand she held a half-eaten burger, and in the other were Rodney's old clothes, neatly folded.

"Thanks for the disguise," she said, and handed over the clothes.

Rodney told her she was welcome and stowed them under his seat along with his kazoo. He said, "That burger looks good."

"Come on into the engine room. There's plenty of food. And the engines are hot enough to cook on."

"In a minute," Rodney called over his shoulder. To Grubber Young, he said, "So the *Ship of Amazement* is following us back to the Planetoid of Amazement. But the Starship Club emergency ship is faster, and will arrive a couple of days ahead."

"That's right." Grubber Young switched channels, and the *Ship of Amazement* seemed to jump toward them. "Full magnification," Grubber said.

Rodney looked back at Drum again and saw her fiddling with the milkshake maker. She seemed entirely engrossed.

Quietly, Rodney said, "What about Drum?"

"That's a tough one, all right," Grubber admitted.

"She never acted like this before?"

"Never. She's always been bubbly, but this time she seems to have boiled over." He liked that turn of phrase and he said it again.

"I wonder if it has anything to do with her job."

"You think being a finder is making her crazy?"

Grubber's question caused Rodney to guess that since wearing the yellow sticker with Drum's essence in it he knew more about Drum than Grubber Young did. Grubber probably didn't even know she was searching for that evil thing, whatever it was. "Maybe," said Rodney cautiously.

"Whatever it is," Grubber said, "if she doesn't straighten out when we get back to the Planetoid of Amazement, I'll have to do something drastic."

They went into the engine room and watched a couple of burger patties snap and bubble as they cooked on what had formerly been the stove and was now outboard engine number one.

Making a burger was easy, and even fries were mainly a matter of lifting the basket out of the hot fat at the right moment. Shakes, however, were more complicated. They were chemistry. Before Grubber and Rodney and Drum concocted anything even remotely drinkable, their experiments spun sweet gloppy stuff all over the ship. But science triumphed at last. Rodney pronounced their latest attempt as good as any shake he'd ever drank.

Six standard days turned out to be a long time when you were trapped inside a place the size of a diner with nothing but diner food, and nothing to do but listen to a more or less intelligent rug tell you things about the Starship Club.

Rodney thought about practicing his kazoo, but he knew that the sound would have driven Drum crazy. Or crazier. Sometimes, though, Rodney sat on his acceleration couch and held the kazoo in his hands, imagining he could hear the music.

Rodney and Grubber talked a lot, and they discovered that the ship's computer knew some games. But all the games had to do with the goods and services provided by the Starship Club, and they got old pretty quick.

Drum stopped bubbling altogether. Though she was friendly enough, she usually stayed by herself in another part of the ship, looking around, tapping walls, generally acting pretty mysterious.

When she wasn't skulking around the ship, she sat

at one of the tables hunched over a waitress's order pad. For a while she would scribble furiously with one of the pencils she'd found in the drawer of the cash register. Then her mouth would move while she studied what she'd done. More often than not, she'd ball up what she'd just written and stuff it into her kangaroo pocket.

She wouldn't let Rodney or Grubber see what she was doing, but once one of the balled-up order receipts fell out of her pocket and Rodney picked it up. He felt a little guilty about looking at it, but he wouldn't allow that to stop him. He and Grubber had a right to know why Drum was acting so weird, and maybe this would give them a clue.

All over the sheet of paper were mathematical calculations in Mobambi. Arrows pointed from one set of equations to another. Some notations were circled; others were crossed out. All of it looked pretty complicated. Up in one corner, almost unreadable under the scratching out, was the word *Slignathi* followed by a question mark.

Rodney couldn't figure out any of it, but all of it, particularly the Slignathi part, seemed important. When Rodney showed the paper to Grubber, he studied it for a while and said at last, "This has something to do with navigation."

"To where?"

"I'm not sure. I'm not much of a navigator."

"How do you find your way around the galaxy?"

"The truth is, Rodney, the ship usually does most of the work."

Rodney nodded and said, "Then this must have to do with a place where the ship doesn't normally go."

They both stared at the paper for a while, but nothing leaped off the page at either of them. Rodney said, "What about that *Slignathi?*" He tapped the word with a finger.

Grubber shook his head and looked worried. "I don't know, Rodney," he said. "I think I liked Drum better when she laughed all the time."

The next time they all sat down to eat together, Grubber took the paper from a pocket in his utility belt and flattened it in the center of the table. After her initial surprise at seeing it, Drum tried to pretend it wasn't there, but she kept glancing at it. Grubber and Rodney kept glancing at her.

Drum said, "What is that?" She flicked the paper with a finger.

"We were hoping you would tell us," Grubber said.

After a moment, Drum laughed. "I really faked you guys out," she said. "It's a shopping list."

"Oh?" said Grubber.

"Sure. Stuff we need for the House of Amazement." She picked up the paper and pointed at things on it. "See? We need a binger bomb, and a torming ring, and maybe a couple of slix."

Rodney didn't see. The stuff Drum pointed to just looked like equations and crossed-out equations.

"Look," said Grubber, "we're your friends, and if you have a problem—"

Angrily, Drum said, "If you're my friends, get off my back." She threw down the remains of her burger and stomped away. The cramped space inside the *Cosmic Ray* would not allow her to go far, but she did the best she could.

"What do we do now?" Rodney said.

"We can't do anything while we're in transit. Once we get to Hutzenklutz Station. . . ." Grubber shrugged.

Late on Day Two, the blue-carpet creature showed them a catalog of Starship Club ships. Drum watched with her arms folded but said nothing. After the first five or six ships, Grubber said, "I know all this stuff," and went off to play one-thumb with the computer— a game Rodney never understood, let alone mastered.

But Rodney was fascinated by the catalog. Some of the ships looked like insects or fish or seed pods. Others looked like hats or hubcaps or kitchen implements. Some looked like no more than lengths of pipe. A few were so totally alien it was difficult for Rodney to see any logic to them at all. Watching the ships go by was like looking into a kaleidoscope.

About Day Three Rodney asked Grubber to show him how to pilot the *Cosmic Ray*.

"Not much to know, actually," Grubber said. "As I said, these Starship Club babies just about run themselves."

"There must be something."

So Grubber showed him. Piloting a Starship Club ship was like driving a car, except for that third dimension. If your destination was on the list in the navigational computer, all you had to do was punch in the code. If you could see a destination, you could fly to it. The ship wouldn't allow you to crash into anything.

Still, turning the knobs and flicking the switches was fun. Rodney felt like a real space cadet. He even learned a few easy tricks of celestial navigation before Grubber got bored with the teaching process.

Grubber sat like a toad for a minute and then said, "Here's something interesting." He turned a knob down to zero, and suddenly Rodney felt terribly dizzy. "Wha—?" he said and floated to the ceiling of the cabin, where he bumped his head. "I'm going to be sick," Rodney said.

"I'll turn the gravity up a few notches."

Grubber turned the knob and Rodney drifted back to the floor. He still didn't weigh more than a hummingbird, but he felt better weighing anything. He found that he could push off with one toe and float all the way across the room. He could do spectacular acrobatics he never would have attempted on Earth. Grubber instructed the computer to play music. Drum came over and danced with Rodney. As they twirled, she laughed the way she had when Rodney first met her, but when the music ended, she went off to be weird again.

"Want to try zero-G one more time?" Grubber said.

Rodney didn't want to, so Grubber turned the gravity up to Earth-normal again. For a while Rodney felt like a lump of lead.

By Day Six Rodney could actually see Hutzenklutz Station—sometimes known as the Planetoid of Amazement—growing in the forward viewscreen. From this distance it looked like a chunk of rock. They got closer and it still looked like a chunk of rock.

Grubber turned up the magnification and pointed out a dome on what was otherwise a barren outcropping. It glinted in the light of Hutzenklutz Station's sun, Alpha Romeo. "That's the House of Amazement. And look there," Grubber said excitedly. "There's Finigle's Last Chance Bar." From this distance, Finigle's Last Chance Bar looked like a tiny soap bubble cozied up against the much larger bubble of the House of Amazement. Grubber went on, "Mara will have the Slignathi's own surprise when she finds out what's been going on."

They had nothing to do, even as the ship came in for a landing. The programming in the blue membership card took care of everything. The domes began to look like half-buried pearls as the horizon of the planetoid flattened and the ship dropped toward the outcropping of rock. Except for the two domes, the planetoid seemed deserted—there was nothing but crags and shadows.

From where the coffee urn had been, the blue-carpet creature was winding up its sales pitch with a dramatic rendition of the Starship Club anthem complete with full orchestra and chorus:

No matter where you are!
Traveling near and far!
On planet or on star!
Remember the blue card will save you trouble!
Trust the Starship Club for help on the double!
Trust the Starship Club for help on the double!

Next to the bigger dome was an enormous flat square area. Lights flashed in sequence around its edge. The *Cosmic Ray* followed a line of lights right into the center of the huge area. At the end of the line of lights was a thing like a Christmas tree, spinning and blinking.

The ship bumped once against the ground, then

bounced around as it skidded. For a moment Rodney thought they were going to skid right past the pearly domes and the big Christmas tree thing and right over the edge of the outcropping. Then he was afraid that they were going to crash into the big dome. But the *Cosmic Ray* slowed and stopped with its flashing red nose a hand's breadth from the tree.

The tree went dark at the same moment the blue-carpet creature finished the last note of its song.

Rodney and the others just sat there for a moment, enjoying the idea of being at Hutzenklutz Station. Rodney was, if anything, even more excited than they were. He was on a genuine alien planetoid!

Hutzenklutz Station, or the Planetoid of Amazement, looked a lot like photographs and paintings Rodney had seen of the moon. Except for the landing lights, there was no color anywhere, but Rodney didn't miss it because there were a million shades of gray. Mountains stood all around, high and sharp enough to poke holes in the black starry sky; the shadows looked as if they'd been cut from black construction paper. To one side, the domes waited. Rainbows ran and twisted on them as if their surfaces were covered with a thin film of oil. Alpha Romeo blazed above it all like a big flare.

Something clanged against the side of the ship, and suddenly they were all moving around collecting their stuff, kind of saying good-bye to the *Cosmic Ray*. Rodney picked up his kazoo and zipped it into the pocket of his jacket. He contemplated the pile of his clothes Drum had worn and then picked them up too. He might need a change.

Drum raised the window between the kitchen— now the engine room—and the rest of the diner and picked up the blue membership card. She kissed it and put it into her pocket.

Grubber pushed a button and turned a knob, and the main hatch fell open. Outside was a short stairway leading down into the ground. "Let's go," said Grubber like a father trying to get his kids off a bus. He marched down the stairs, and Drum followed. Rodney came last.

They were in a low man-made, or at least creature-made, tunnel. Grubber stopped at a small control console and flicked it on. In the air over the console a three-dimensional picture of the landing field solidified. Grubber set dials and turned switches. A moment later, a pylon rose at each corner of the landing field. They looked like barber poles, even to the white globes on top. Grubber threw a throttle and the white globes began to glow.

"That should take care of Grits. Now all we have to do is wait," Grubber said. He set off down the tunnel.

13

The Terrible Truth

"What happens to the *Cosmic Ray* now?" Rodney asked as he hurried to keep up.

"We can either buy it cheap," Grubber said, "or a couple of guys from the Starship Club will eventually come out to get it."

Grubber and Drum walked pretty briskly. The air was cool and had a strange, but not unpleasant, smell. It was alien air. Rodney took a big lungful.

Soon they came to an area where the walls were decorated with mosaics of aliens and alien ships, each identified in Mobambi. On the last wall, the red tile made letters that spelled out WELCOME TO THE PLANETOID OF AMAZEMENT: THE MOST AMAZING EXHIBIT IN THE UNIVERSE.

They walked through a turnstile and entered a small elevator. It smelled dead, as if the air had been boxed up inside for a long time. Around the top of the car were cardboard signs, each of which had words and a simple drawing advertising such exhibits as RAY GUNS OF MYSTERY and THE SPACE SUIT OF DOOM and THE PARADE OF SHIIPS OF ALL PLANETS. Each card looked as if it had been drawn with a big marking pen by a kid.

Rodney found the amateurishness and cheapness of the cards embarrassing, and he tried not to look at them. If they were any indication, the House of Amazement might not be "the most amazing exhibition in the universe."

If Grubber had lied about that, who knew what else he might be lying about? And what about Drum? Even if Grubber was just the lovable looney he appeared to be, Drum seemed to have big secrets. Rodney advised himself to stay alert, and congratulated himself on having learned how to fly the *Cosmic Ray.*

After years of seeing people on *Star Trek* talk to their elevator, Rodney was surprised when Grubber had to start his by pushing a button. A buzzer sounded, the doors closed, and the car went up so quickly that Rodney left his stomach behind. It was the first time since the adventure began that Rodney had felt discomfort aboard a moving alien vehicle.

Nobody said anything during the ride, so Rodney had plenty of time to wonder about all the strange and extraordinary things he would see when the elevator doors opened. Maybe he was making too much of those hand-drawn signs. Grubber probably just thought they were cute.

The elevator stopped suddenly and his stomach caught up. The doors opened and he saw—

Well, Rodney hadn't known what to expect, but this wasn't it. He looked across a hallway and over another turnstile at a room about the size of his living room at home. It was painted what was now a faded yellow. A big brown water spot had been spreading for years up near one corner. Two long fluorescent light fixtures hung from cracked acoustical tile over long glass cases.

Rodney could not see from the elevator what was in the cases. But hanging from the walls were pictures, some of them three-dimensional, of strange creatures with big eyes and tiny bodies, a sneering guy wearing a white fringed suit covered in sparkling gems, and what looked like a bullfighter with six arms.

Models of alien spaceships and flying creatures floated near the ceiling. At first Rodney thought the models were held aloft by antigravity rays; but when he looked closely, Rodney could see that each of them was suspended from thin silvery wires.

The back wall of the room was a single picture window that looked out into the big dome, the biggest enclosed space Rodney had ever seen. It was strange looking across what seemed to be miles of field to the pale rainbow surface of the opposite dome wall. On the field were more spaceships, but

Rodney didn't think these were models. He couldn't even see all of the ship nearest the window, just a fin with a strange design on it.

"Welcome, welcome to the House of Amazement," Grubber said as he stepped off the elevator. Somewhere a scratching noise began and then a very old recording of Grubber's voice said, "Welcome, welcome to the House of Amazement. Admission is three credits. Admission to the Parade of Ships of All Planets is one credit more. Please deposit your money—" By this time, Grubber had crossed the hallway to flick a switch behind a small door in the wall. He was smiling with embarrassment at Rodney. "No charge for personal friends of the management," he said.

He led them through the exhibit room, and in the cases Rodney saw a lot of interesting machinery and bones and rocks and other bits of stuff. Grubber stopped and faced his exhibits proudly. He hit himself in the chest with the flat of his hand and sighed. He said, "Well, Rodney, what do you think?"

Rodney didn't know what to say. On the one hand, if Grubber wasn't entirely crazy, he had to realize that the reality of the House of Amazement was nothing like the stories he'd told back on Earth. It was less like an interstellar Disneyland than it was like one of those roadside attractions in the desert that had a few rocks, a stuffed snake, and a soft-drink machine, and called itself a museum.

On the other hand, if Grubber was anything like a human, he had an enormous capacity to kid himself. Maybe over the years he'd convinced himself that everything he said about the House of Amazement was true. If that was the case, was it Rodney's job to give him the bad news?

Rodney glanced at Drum for a cue. Drum gave a small shake of her head. Rodney said, "It's real interesting, isn't it! You and Drum must have worked very hard collecting all this stuff." So far, Rodney had not been forced to lie.

"Hey, you know? I do the best I can with what I have."

"I guess you—"

"Yes," Grubber went on, "it's not easy running a first-class attraction out here at the edge of nowhere. You have to use your ingenuity. You have to make do."

"You have to make things up," Drum said solemnly.

"Well, yeah," Grubber said. He and Drum laughed together.

"I guess advertising is important," Rodney said. He was relieved that Grubber and Drum did not take themselves or their attraction too seriously.

"Image," said Grubber with a finger in the air, "is

everything." He turned and quickly led Rodney and Drum into a side room that contained a bed and a desk and a few chairs.

Rodney said, "What do regular tourists say when they see this place?"

"Depends," Grubber said. "Sometimes they get into it."

"Sometimes they want their money back," Drum said.

Grubber winked. "We don't lose many."

In the side room, magazines and papers were stacked between the desk and the bed. Additional natural and mechanical bits—unsorted exhibits?—were scattered everywhere. Gears and machine housings were laid out on the desk. Something brown and wrinkled stood on the top of one pile and gave off an incredible skunklike odor. If it hadn't been for the odor, Rodney would have thought it was a very old apple.

On his way through Grubber kicked things aside without regard for what they were. Stacks of magazines fell over into long glossy drifts. A few things Rodney had thought were machine parts skittered across the floor under their own power, then settled in corners as if they had never moved.

Another bed was in a small room where more magazines were stacked against the wall along with floppy disks, boxes of insectlike electronic parts, squares of what looked like plastic Graham crackers, and chiseled marble slabs. On a pedestal next to the bed was a black beachball with three big holes in it.

Grubber loosened a rope that was belayed around a cleat in the wall and lowered an enormous feather to the floor. He pushed his open hand against the feather as if testing a mattress. "You'll be comfortable in here with Drum," he said. "The brain of an Anabumpopest bimbo is the lightest, softest thing around here."

"Looks good," Rodney said, and touched the feather. He was trying to act nonchalant. But the fact was, despite his disappointment at the shoddyness of the House of Amazement, Rodney could not help being excited. He had been around long enough to know that things were not always what they appeared to be—the diner, for one; maybe Drum, for another—and anyway, here he was on an alien planetoid. He didn't want to quibble.

Rubbing his hands together, Grubber walked out of the room again. "I can't wait to see the look on Mara's face when she finds out we've been to Earth."

"But Earth isn't really the Legendary Treasure Planet," Rodney said.

"Mara doesn't know that," Grubber said over his shoulder.

After Rodney stowed his kazoo, Drum led him through the museum again, along the hallway past where the elevator still waited, and came to a slit in the wall as tall as a person. "Just squeeze on through," Drum said as she forced herself into the slit, making a noise that sounded as if she were stroking corduroy pants. Rodney followed. The noise sounded much louder as he went through, feeling as if he were squeezing between two fat people.

The other side of the slit was darker than the House of Amazement, and in the cool air, strange almost-sweet smells dragged at Rodney's nose. Great winged things hung from the ceiling. Some looked as if they could fly; others looked like big flightless birds—penguins, maybe. If Leonardo da Vinci had been from Mars, Rodney thought, this is the kind of stuff he might have designed. And though the pieces didn't seem to be in any order, the confusion was interesting. Rodney felt sure an interior decorator had been involved.

Rusting wheels and levers and springs rested on the ceiling beams. Star charts and paintings of planets covered the walls. One painting featured a ball of fur with hundreds of sticklike legs. Beneath it were the words EARTH PERSON. ARTIST'S CONCEPTION.

"This," said Drum, "is Finigle's Last Chance Bar. As you can see, Mara has had it decorated with artifacts that are supposed to come from Earth, the Legendary Treasure Planet." She seemed normal again. Maybe the itch to find that evil thing didn't bother her once she got home.

"I don't recognize any of it."

"I'm not surprised. Until the *Vagabond Lover III* arrived, nobody knew where Earth was."

"Nobody except Sak Nussemm, the guy who took the picture of the *Woman Flagging Down a Bus*."

"He knew where the earth was," Drum said, "but he refused to tell anybody." She shook her head. "From everything I hear, Old Sak was even crazier than Grits. As far as most people were concerned, his picture was a fake, just one more artist's conception."

"And then you and Grubber saw that it matched the picture on the probe."

"Right. That's what started us thinking that maybe Old Sak really had something. With the help of the Starship Club we figured out the location of the planet the probe came from and went to have a look for ourselves."

Something was wrong with what Drum was telling him. Rodney said, "Wait a minute. You didn't need old Sak, or the probe either. The Starship Club put an emergency ship on Earth. Why not ask them where it was?"

"Well, actually, Grubber and Mara, and I suppose a

lot of other treasure hunters, thought of doing that. Then we discovered the terrible truth."

"Terrible truth?"

"Yeah." Drum stuck both her hands into her kangaroo pocket and went on as if she were talking to the picture of the ball of fur. She said, "The Starship Club causes emergency ships to be built on a lot of planets, and they don't often trouble to find out what the locals call their particular ball of dirt. As far as the Starship Club is concerned, Earth doesn't exist. The planet where you live is just another serial number in their catalog."

Rodney was shocked. His home planet was just one more dirt ball in a staggeringly large galaxy full of dirt balls. There was no point being offended, but he could not help feeling disoriented and sad at the sudden reduction of Earth's importance. "Oh," he said.

Big, gruff laughter exploded from the other room. Drum smiled broadly. "Come on," she said. "We don't want to miss any of this." She dragged Rodney—who was still getting a grip on the situation—through an arched doorway into a long room that had a bar down one side and was otherwise full of round wooden disks that floated at table height. More star maps and artists' conceptions—as accurate as the ones Rodney had already seen—hung on the walls.

Grubber and a creature were hugging. They kept

hugging as Rodney and Drum pulled up chairs and sat down. Rodney rested his hand on the table and it didn't wobble. When Grubber and the creature were done calling each other terrible names in Mobambi and slapping each other on the back, Grubber introduced it to Rodney.

The creature was a taller, slimmer version of Grits, with a pinch at the waist. Like Grubber and Drum, Rodney persisted in thinking of her as female despite the fact he knew human concepts probably meant nothing in this case. She wasn't wearing anything, not unless the glowing stuff he'd taken for skin was an outfit of some kind. She was Mara, of course, the owner and operator of Finigle's Last Chance Bar. She and Rodney hooked fingers.

"Drinks all around?" asked Mara.

"Of course," said Grubber expansively. "Put it on my tab."

Mara ran, light-footed, to the bar—her passing would not have crushed dandelions—and leaped over it, expending no more effort than Rodney might use jumping over a crack in the pavement. She set up three glasses on the bar as Grubber, Rodney, and Drum bellied up. Into Grubber's empty glass she dropped a blue paper umbrella; then she gave Rodney and Drum each a green plastic mermaid.

Grubber sucked on the end of his umbrella, nodded

and smacked his lips, then broke the umbrella in two as if it were an egg and let ice tumble into the glass, followed by sparkling blue liquid. Rodney broke open his plastic mermaid and smoky green stuff settled at the bottom of his glass like fog. Rodney took a sip. The fog tasted something like cinnamon toast and even crunched a little, though he couldn't find any solid places with his tongue.

Drum drank her green smoke, slapped Rodney on the shoulder, and smiled as she nodded in the direction of the other two.

Grubber leaned casually across the bar. "How's business?" he said to Mara, who was folding glasses and putting them away.

"A little slow. Can't complain. And yourself?"

"The usual. Drum's a good finder."

"Yep." There was a long silence during which Grubber stared into his drink and Mara set a spongy thing the shape of a meatloaf on the bar. As she stroked the meatloaf, it purred, and any liquid that had been spilled on the bar began to crawl toward it in long snakes. She said, "She find anything interesting?"

Drum didn't seem to be paying any attention to the conversation, but when Rodney looked in her direction, she winked.

So casually it hurt, Grubber said, "Well, there's Rodney here, of course."

"Oh?"

Grubber Young stirred his drink with the handle of the broken umbrella. He said, "Yeah. He's from kind of an interesting little planet."

Mara stopped stroking the meatloaf and said, "Um."

"Yes," said Grubber. "Lots of interesting artifacts." He showed her the three-dimensional picture of the Statue of Liberty.

She said, "This is the famous *Woman Flagging Down a Bus.*"

"Right."

Mara's hands began to shake. In a fearfully quiet voice, she said, "Rodney's from Earth? The Legendary Treasure Planet?"

"Well—" Rodney began, but stopped when Drum put her hand on his arm and Grubber shot him an angry look.

Mara glanced in Rodney's direction, and her huge lidless eyes narrowed. She said, "And what does Rodney think of my little collection of Earth memorabilia?"

Rodney said, "Collecting all this stuff must have been a lot of work."

"Not really. Grits is a good finder too." She glared again at Grubber Young and said, "Where exactly is Grits?"

"How should I know?" Grubber said, and chuckled. "I expect he'll be along."

152

Pressing on, Mara said, "Rodney doesn't look anything like any artist's conception of an Earthperson I've ever seen. Sure you weren't on the wrong planet?"

Grubber chuckled again, and drained his drink. He stood up but didn't move away from the bar.

Mara said, "How do you know it's Earth? Nobody knows where it is."

"It's Earth," Grubber said.

"The Legendary Treasure Planet?" Mara said.

Grubber just smiled.

Mara said, "Rodney, you and I will have to talk a little."

"He doesn't know where it is from here," Drum said. "He was just a passenger."

"We all were," Grubber said. "And the navigational computer aboard the Starship Club ship we rode in on has probably randomized itself by now."

With exaggerated care, Mara put the meatloaf thing under the bar. She looked at Grubber for a moment, then, in a low, threatening tone, said, "You might as well tell me where the LTP is. You can't possibly use all the treasure yourself. You don't have the room."

"My," said Grubber, "what a menacing attitude we have. Come on. Drum, you can show Rodney around."

The three of them walked out through the arched doorway, and Mara called, "See you soon, Rodney!"

As Grubber dragged him along, Rodney called over his shoulder, "Let's do lunch!" In a much quieter voice, Rodney said, "Just how desperate is she?"

"You call that desperation?" Grubber Young said. "You haven't seen Mara desperate. Not yet."

"Just be careful, that's all," Drum said.

14
Which Is Which?

Back in his room, Grubber threw the evil-smelling apple thing at a target on the wall. The apple went right through without making a hole, though the skunk smell lingered. Grubber lifted a crate onto his desk and sorted through the bits of cloth and metal. He held up a pink egg the size of a basketball. Tiny lights hurried about inside it. Grubber frowned at it with his eyebrows together. "What does this look like to you?"

"Maybe a dynamo of some kind," Drum said.

Rodney said, "Looks to me like a cage for fairies."

Grubber frowned at the egg for a moment longer, then smiled. "I like it," he said. "Drum, make up a card that says this thing is a fairy cage from Cambaxus III."

"I could be wrong," Rodney said.

"It's almost certain," Grubber said as he puzzled over a black brick that jingled when he shook it. "But the universe is a big place, and chances are good none of my customers will know the difference. If they do know the difference, we'll apologize and change the card. The card, Drum."

Rodney followed Drum into her room. Drum stuck her head up inside the black beachball and put her hands into the holes up to her wrists, and a few seconds later a card protruded from the side of the machine; in Mobambi, it said that this was a fairy cage from Cambaxus III, used by the natives to store stray luck.

"Not bad, huh?"

Rodney looked at the card and said, "Is anything out there what the label says it is?"

Drum said, "A few things. But to tell the truth, Rodney, I forget which is which." In the other room she set the card on the desk next to Grubber, who was now looking at a thin, smooth sheet of metal that stretched like rubber until the words EVOLUTION: IS IT REALLY FOR EVERYBODY? appeared. When Grubber let it spring back, the words disappeared.

"Advertising?" Rodney said.

Grubber shook his head. "Naw. Somebody else's cockamamie religion is always more interesting than somebody else's cockamamie advertising. I'd say it's from the Casowari cult of Tramps-Gidney 23. They've been trying to get their main god to answer this question for thousands of years."

"Really?" Rodney said.

Grubber shrugged and threw the sheet aside.

Drum said, "I'm going to show Rodney around, okay?"

"Be careful. We don't want Mara talking to him."

"Right."

Out in the main exhibit room, Drum guided Rodney up and down the showcases. In each one were small, strange bits. Some of them looked like rock samples. Others could have come off Earthly automobiles, or out of gadget drawers in Earthly kitchens. A whole case of pistols, radios, and sensing devices looked like props from movies or TV shows Rodney had seen. Only a few items looked genuinely alien. Rodney had no idea what they were, and he knew he could not trust the identification cards. Everything was dusty, and most cases had dead insects curled up in the corners.

The whole production was so cheap-looking and idiotic that Rodney wondered if the entire Planetoid of Amazement wasn't a front for something more sinister. He refused to be lulled into believing that the Earth was safe.

They turned away from the case and almost ran into Mara. "Hi, Drum," she said pleasantly. "Hi, Rodney."

"Hi, Mara," Drum said. They walked toward the doorway and Mara leaped over them, blocking their way. She put her arm through Rodney's and led him toward Finigle's Last Chance Bar. "We have a lot to talk about, honey. And the drinks are on me."

Drum grabbed Rodney's other arm and said, "Not now, Mara. We haven't finished our tour."

Rodney thought the two were going to pull him apart. "Hey look," Rodney said, "I'll show you some Legendary Treasure." He got free of Drum's grip and pulled a coin from his pocket.

"What is it?" Mara said without letting go.

"We on Earth call it a nickel. Find a few of these babies and you'll be rich."

Eagerly, Mara said, "Let me see," and put out her hand.

Rodney held up the nickel and dropped it. "Oops," he said as it rolled across the exhibit room floor. Mara scampered after it.

"Which way?" Rodney whispered.

Drum ran down a hallway Rodney had not yet been in and out onto the domed field of spaceships.

"Pretty clever," Drum said.

"Yeah, I guess it was," Rodney said, feeling pleased with himself. His escape from Mara seemed too easy to be called daring, yet perhaps that was the nature of daring escapes once they were successfully completed. He needed more experience.

"Your parents would be proud."

Rodney turned on Drum and said, "Look, Drum. This is *my* adventure, okay?"

"So far," Drum said, and set off across the field.

"What do you mean, 'so far'?" Rodney called after her. He walked fast to keep up.

"You don't have a lock on adventures any more than your parents do."

"I know that—"

Drum stopped and faced Rodney. "And let me tell you something else: Having an adventure is not a kid's game. It can be dangerous."

"Are you having an adventure like that?" Rodney said excitedly.

"Soon. Maybe." She set off again and refused to say more.

Hundreds of ships rested on the field; it had been scorched, blackened, and pulverized by spaceship exhaust. Some of the ships looked as if they'd been snapped together out of plastic building blocks. Others were sleek bulbous fruits, as if they were designed to move through atmosphere as well as vacuum. One looked like a porcupine made of metal pipes. Near each ship floated a sign in Mobambi.

Rodney recognized the place from the dream given to him by the yellow sticker. He could read the floating signs now. Normally being here would have excited Rodney, but he'd been excited for so long—since meeting Grubber and Drum—that being on this field looking at these ships was just one more wonder.

"This is the Parade of Ships of All Planets," Drum said. "Seeing it usually costs an extra credit."

Rodney said, "Is the *Vagabond Lover III* here?"

"Of course." Drum guided Rodney through a forest of tall ships, each of which looked like a spray of frozen water, and then along a row of giant metal insects. In the middle of it, Rodney recognized the *Vagabond Lover III* from the picture in the *Encyclopedia Cafeteria*. He just stared.

The probe had long arms pointing in different directions, and an array of dish antennae all attached to an open metal framework. It had no legs, and the framework looked a little crushed. The *Vagabond Lover III* obviously was never meant to rest on the ground.

"Here," said Drum. She tapped a metal plate welded to one side.

Rodney had forgotten Drum was there. He joined her. The plate she tapped was gold, or gold colored anyway. Etched into it were the originals of the messages Grubber Young had shown to Rodney. They were big enough to see without a magnifier. Among the greetings and the challenges and the mathematical formulae was the name Watson Congruent and his address. Rodney's address.

"Wow," Rodney said.

Drum let Rodney stand there and marvel for a

while, and then she said, "Come on. I have some stuff to check." Rodney let himself be pulled away, but he kept looking back. He wanted to remember every line of the probe. Drum walked ahead of him.

"What kind of stuff?" Rodney asked, as he hurried to catch up.

"Stuff," said Drum pointedly.

They eventually came to a ship that looked like an igloo. The floating sign said it was a scout ship from Timbuck Two. Among this collection there was nothing special about the ship, but it seemed to interest Drum greatly. She and Rodney climbed inside through a complicated airlock that reminded him of a drawbridge.

Inside the ship the walls and floors were faced with colored plastic planks. In the center of the main room was a round table. Drum touched a few of the planks, and they changed color. She gripped a pole stuck into the round table and turned it slightly.

"What's special about a ship from Timbuck Two?"

"Just routine maintenance," Drum said without looking at him.

"Maintenance on a ship that'll never have to fly again?"

Drum glanced at Rodney but did not say anything as she continued to make adjustments.

"Does this have anything to do with why you acted

so weird aboard the *Cosmic Ray*? Does it have anything to do with your search for the evil thing?"

With both hands Drum grabbed a glass mushroom and pulled it up no more than an inch, causing a blue plastic cracker to protrude from the top. She took the cracker and quickly hid it in her kangaroo pocket. Sounding guilty, she said, "What is that supposed to mean?"

"I don't know," said Rodney. He remembered how strong Drum's grip had been when she caught him trying to use the Chocolatron Hotline, and he was suddenly aware that Drum was not just a rational being but a talking kangaroo with sharp claws and teeth. Despite his newborn apprehension, he said, "I picked up some impressions from that yellow sticker."

Drum gauged Rodney with her eyes and said, "Forget about them, Rodney. They have nothing to do with you."

Not knowing how far he could push her, Rodney said, "That's not an answer. Maybe I can help."

"Give me a break, will you, Rodney?" Drum stalked out of the ship.

Rodney followed as quickly as he could. Drum was hiding something. And the fact that Grubber didn't seem to know what it was either made the whole situation even more mysterious. Rodney refused to feel guilty for asking questions, though he could not help being cautious. He caught up with Drum halfway down the row of ships.

A few steps later, Drum said, "Sorry I exploded back there."

"That's okay."

"I have a lot on my mind. If Earth isn't the Legendary Treasure Planet, Grubber will get itchy to hunt for it again, and I have no idea where to begin."

"Tough being a finder." Rodney didn't buy Drum's explanation for a minute, but he couldn't forget the strong grasp of her hand around his wrist.

"Yeah."

They went back into the House of Amazement, watching for Mara, but evidently she'd gone back to Finigle's Last Chance Bar. They went down in the elevator and back along the hallway with the mosaics on it. Drum adjusted the controls, and they walked up the stairs to the Cosmic Ray.

It was just as they'd left it. A smell of cooking grease lingered, making Rodney's mouth water. Rodney knew it was odd, but he felt as if he were visiting his home.

Drum made a drawer in the side of the computer—what had been the lunch counter—slide open, then took the blue plastic cracker from her kangaroo pocket. She set the cracker into the drawer, where it fit perfectly, and pushed the drawer closed. She pressed some buttons on the drawer, making the lights flash in a way that satisfied her.

They left the *Cosmic Ray* and went back to the House of Amazement. "What did you do?" Rodney asked.

"It's kind of technical," Drum said.

It was obvious that this answer called for more questions, but Rodney kept silent. He didn't want to give her the chance to say something evasive again.

In his room, Grubber was still sorting junk. He held up something that looked like a chicken leg without feathers and said, "What do you think this is?"

Before Rodney or Drum could answer, a noise began. It sounded as if somebody were dumping a load of gravel on the roof. A voice came through the gravel. It said, "*Ship of Amazement* calling Hutzenklutz Station. *Ship of Amazement* calling Hutzenklutz Station."

Drum said, "It's Grits."

Grubber Young said, "Now we'll have some fun." He threw the chicken leg aside and ran from the room.

15

Parley with Rattlesnakes

While riding the elevator to the top of Hutzenklutz Station, Grubber Young spoke as if he were lecturing to paying customers: "What you are about to witness is positively one of the most amazing things here on the Planetoid of Amazement—the dowsers and controls of many races cobbled together to make a flight-monitoring and guidance system second to none." He winked at Rodney and said in a normal voice, "I built it myself."

The elevator door opened onto a tower room with windows all around. Outside were the domes of the Parade of Ships of All Planets and Finigle's Last Chance Bar. On the other side was the vast expanse of the landing field. Rodney could see the *Cosmic Ray*. The Christmas tree thing had moved and was flashing again.

Inside, below the windows, were machines. Some of them looked like control stations on Earth. Others were incomprehensible to Rodney. No two were the same. Lights winked on most of them. Some had video screens. On others, parts wigwagged or jumped or crawled up and back. The room looked something like the corner window of a major department store at Christmas.

"All this works together?" Rodney said.

"He didn't say it all works," Drum said. "He just said he built it himself."

Evidently, Grubber's verbal explanations could be as reliable as the cards explaining his exhibits. While the lights flashed and parts moved, Rodney realized that the sound of gravel hitting the roof was really radio static. There seemed to be less of it now, and Grits could be heard much more clearly.

Mara was leaning against a slanting board before one of the stranger control panels. Colored eggs orbited inside a thing that looked like an old-fashioned birdcage while she turned it this way and that. She balanced the cage on one finger while she glared at Grubber, Rodney, and Drum.

"I told you he'd show up," Grubber said.

Mara turned her back on them. Grubber just smiled.

Grits went on. ". . . and them consarned bushwackers blew up my ship and I almost didn't escape with my life. But that Earth is the Legendary Treasure Planet, sure enough. I seen the *Woman Flagging Down a Bus* my very own self."

"Can you find your way back?" Mara said.

"Sure as shooting. Just as soon as I settle my score with them two desperados."

Grubber and Drum nudged each other. They didn't look worried. Though Rodney didn't want to see *anybody* killed, he was relieved that Grits didn't consider *him* important enough to be a target.

A bright star detached itself from the background of stars and got bigger. Soon, it became a front-loading washing machine. It was the *Ship of Amazement*.

Mara said, "If I were you, I'd either prepare for an unpleasant death or get out of here. I'm not sure I can control Grits."

"Thanks for the warning," Grubber said, and laughed.

Mara looked at them for a moment, then turned to watch the *Ship of Amazement* land.

Only it didn't land. It was dropping toward the landing field when suddenly it bounced so high, Rodney could no longer see the ship from where he stood. "Tarnation!" Grits cried.

"What?" Mara said.

"What was what?" Grubber said. He and Drum were falling all over each other trying to keep from laughing.

Grits called, "What's going on? I can see the field but I can't get near it."

The *Ship of Amazement* dropped again, and once

167

more bounced away. Grits cried, "Tarnation!" again.

Grubber strolled to a control panel that looked like the ones aboard his ship. He made a few adjustments and said, "Hi there, Grits."

"Let me down," Grits cried.

Grubber said, "First you have to promise me something."

"I don't parley with rattlesnakes."

The ship bounced again and Grits cried out.

Mara said, "I don't appreciate the way you're treating my employee."

"A little more respect, Grubber," Drum said.

"Of course," Grubber said. "First you have to promise me something, *Mister* Grits."

The ship bounced again and Grits called, "Spit it out, Grubber."

"Before I'll let you land," Grubber said, "you have to promise not to try killing me and Drum."

"Horsefeathers," Grits snapped.

Grubber said nothing but let the ship bounce again.

"Wait a minute," Mara said. She pointed out at the field and said, "I thought you got rid of that space navy surplus trampoline force field."

"You mean the iterative retrofluxion multi-impact elastic field transponder?"

Mara said, "Hah!" and twirled her birdcage. When it stopped spinning, she reached in and pulled out the one egg that was glowing. She cracked it open and the shell evaporated into nothing, leaving behind a plastic jigger Rodney immediately identified as a dart gun. It looked like a plastic toy somebody might buy in a dime store. It was loaded with a dart tipped with a rubber suction cup.

The *Ship of Amazement* continued to bounce. Grits groaned.

Grubber said, "You can't use that." Now he sounded worried. Drum appeared worried too. Rodney looked at Mara. Her face was set in a stubborn grimace.

"I can and I will if you don't turn that trampoline field off."

"She's bluffing," Grubber said lightly. "She could blow the entire planetoid out of orbit with that weapon of hers."

"Bluffing, am I?" Mara said. She fired the dart gun at the window overlooking the landing field. The rubber-tipped dart stuck with a *thunk*, and a cone of light shot from it. The light shone through the thickness of the window and out into the vacuum beyond. In the cone outside the window was a long plank, on which a rubber band had been pulled back. Loaded into the V of the rubber band was a gigantic paper clip. Plank, rubber band, and paper clip were all sculpted out of bright white light.

"Be reasonable, Mara," Grubber said. "Even if you don't mind killing us all, you ought to respect property rights. I paid good money for those pylons. They belong to me."

"Turn them off, then."

"Not till Grits promises."

Mara aimed the plastic gun, which aimed the paper clip launcher. She pulled the trigger, and the rubber band hurled the paper clip at a white globe atop one of the pylons. None of this made any noise, which seemed pretty strange despite the fact Rodney knew it was because there was no air in space to conduct sound. The paper clip struck its target, and the pylon exploded into white sparks. That didn't make any noise either.

But at the same moment as the globe exploded the ground shook violently. Grubber and Drum were wide-eyed. Rodney could feel his heart pounding on the wall of his chest. The building creaked, settling.

The next time the *Ship of Amazement* bounced, it came a lot closer to the ground.

"Turn the field off," Mara said.

Grubber cocked his head at Drum and said, "Do you think he'll kill us?" He didn't sound as assured as he had formerly.

"He has to catch us first," Drum said.

Mara had time to line up another shot while Grubber considered his angles. Rodney was about ready to shout at him when Grubber said, "Right." He made adjustments on his control panel, and the remaining three white globes went dark.

The *Ship of Amazement* dropped like a rock and struck the landing field so hard that Rodney could feel the impact through his feet, though it didn't shake him up as much as the explosion had. Everybody ran to the window. The ship rested on a flattened corner, but aside from that it did not seem to be damaged. The Christmas tree thing moved toward the ship like a periscope through water and stopped near it.

"Grits," Mara called into her birdcage.

It was a long few seconds until Grits said, "What do you want?"

"Are you all right?"

"Not entirely. I got a powerful thirst."

"Come on in," Grubber said. "I'll buy you a drink."

"I won't drink with a man who tried to kill me."

"It was a mistake, Grits. A mistake."

"Come on in, Grits," said Mara. "We'll talk about Earth."

They waited for Grits at the end of the mosaic corridor. It took him so long to appear that Mara eventually went to see if he was really all right. They came back together, with Grits leaning heavily on Mara's arm. There was a smudge across his forehead and he was limping, but Rodney didn't know how much of that was theater and how much was real.

When Grits saw Grubber Young and Drum, his jaw began to work; he pulled out his pistol and leveled it at them. "An accident, huh?" he said.

"I'm real sorry," Grubber said. The serious expression on his face had the professional look of an undertaker's.

"Hah," Grits said with raucous contempt.

Grubber opened his hands at his sides and said, "I couldn't be any more sincere if I were wearing a tie."

Mara said, "Grits would be a lot more forgiving if you'd tell us about Earth."

"I guess we owe you that much," Grubber said, making Drum look at him with surprise.

Grits dismissed Grubber with a wave of one hand and said, "You know we can't trust him. I don't know why we even try." He limped into the elevator and waited for them.

Grubber, Drum, Mara, and Grits sat at a floating table in Finigle's Last Chance Bar. Each of them had a glass of blue liquid, and in the center of the table was a cup with a lot of blue paper umbrellas in it. Discreetly seated a table away, Rodney nursed a glass of the green fog that came in plastic mermaids. In the silent bar Rodney had no trouble hearing the wrangling conversation at the next table.

Mara said, "I'm waiting."

"I am too," Grubber said. "I want to know how Grits got away from the Earthman who hustled him out of the diner."

Grits' eyes got more round, and his glow went a little yellow. He fumbled with his fingers and sipped his drink. He mumbled something.

"What?" said Drum, leaning closer.

"I didn't exactly escape," Grits said.

"He let you go?" Grubber said. He liked the idea.

Grits evidently decided to make the best of the situation, so he laughed and slapped the table and said, "Yep. He just said he ain't never had such a good time and let me go. I skedaddled across the field to the *Ship of Amazement* like my pants was on fire, I can tell you."

"You're changing the subject," Mara said darkly.

Grits got ahold of himself, folded his arms, and glared at Grubber Young.

"The truth is," Grubber said, "Earth is a nice place to visit, but it isn't the Legendary Treasure Planet."

He got blank looks from Mara and Grits.

"Isn't that right, Drum?"

"Slignathi's truth," Drum said.

Grits made an impolite noise. Mara might as well have been a statue.

"Isn't that right, Rodney?"

Rodney wasn't sure what was going on, but he said, "Absolutely," and tried to sound sincere.

"Then why did you go there?" Mara said.

"It was the *Vagabond Lover III*," Grubber said. After that, he had to explain about the *Woman Flagging Down a Bus*, and the gold plate, and the address that Watson Congruent, Rodney's father, had paid a quarter to have etched onto it.

"So you just went to say howdy," Grits said.

"That's all," Grubber said. "Earth is not the Legendary Treasure Planet." He said it with such conviction, even Rodney found him difficult to believe.

Mara drummed the fingers of one hand on the table. For the first time, Rodney noticed she had six of them. Her big eyes narrowed, but she wasn't looking at anything in the room. Everybody drank. Grits mumbled under his breath about explosions and rattlesnakes and revenge.

At last Mara said, "If Earth isn't the Legendary Treasure Planet, then it just isn't. We'll have to keep looking." She stood up. Grits stood next to her swaying a little. Maybe he was more shaken by his crash landing than Rodney had thought.

Grubber tried to link fingers with Grits, but Grits would have none of it. As Grubber, Drum, and Rodney left Finigle's Last Chance Bar, Mara and Grits were sitting again, talking with their heads together.

On the other side of the slit door between the bar and the House of Amazement, Grubber put his arm around Drum and pulled her close. He said, "I can guarantee that before this week is out, Mara and Grits will be boosting for Earth."

"Reverse psychology," Rodney said.

"What do you know about reverse psychology?" Grubber said. "It's a Krel invention."

"Not on Earth, it isn't."

Grubber Young let go of Drum and said, "Speaking of Earth, we have to repair the *Ship of Amazement* and take Rodney home."

"No hurry," Rodney said.

"He's having his adventure," Drum said.

As he walked off, Grubber chuckled and said, "You've come to the wrong place if you want adventure. From now on, here on the Planetoid of Amazement, it'll be business as usual."

After Drum followed Grubber back to their rooms, Rodney stood in the doorway of the main exhibit room contemplating the showcases and the Parade of Ships of All Planets beyond. All around, he'd had an exciting time. He'd seen the Planetoid of Amazement and sipped alien beverages. Outsmarting Mara with a nickel had been pretty good. And he'd saved everybody from Grits at least twice. Not bad for a kid without experience.

He hadn't saved the Earth, but Rodney figured he should get points for quality, not just quantity. Besides, he did not trust Grubber and Drum entirely even now. Neither of them seemed to have any qualms about keeping secrets or misleading people. He might yet have a chance to save the Earth. He sighed contentedly. Life was good.

"Rodney," a voice behind him said.

He turned and was confronted by Grits, who was smiling at a secret joke. He said, "Mara wants to talk to you," and flung glitter over Rodney. As the glitter fell, it took the House of Amazement with it, and a moment later new puzzle pieces fell into place, building a scene that Rodney was not happy to see.

16

The Logic of Mara

"Hello, Rodney," Mara said.

Rodney was standing with his limbs spread inside a framework among what looked like springs as thick as somebody's leg. He couldn't move, and the thing restraining him seemed to be a bright cone of white light cast by a single bare light bulb above his head.

The framework was near one end of an oval plot paved with gravel. On all sides grass grew taller than a man and was so tightly packed that Rodney could not see what was beyond. Near Rodney a record was playing on a portable phonograph that rested on a scuffed wooden table. Here and there inside the oval plot, sheets of stone shot up at odd angles, reminding Rodney of ice floes. Chains clanked, doors creaked, and occasionally somebody moaned.

Rodney tried to leave the framework, but the harder he pushed, the more the light pushed back at him. "Where are we?"

"You don't recognize it?" Mara said with concern.

"No," Rodney said carefully. How much should he admit?

"The designer told me this is a typical Earth torture chamber."

Rodney didn't like the sound of that. He said, "Not anywhere on Earth that I know."

"That Grubber! Maybe he was lying when he told me you were from Earth."

"Maybe," Rodney said cautiously.

"He was so convincing that the Earth is not the Legendary Treasure Planet that I didn't believe him for a minute."

"It's not."

"So you say," Mara said. "No matter. We will find out the truth. If you're from Earth, tell me about its riches."

"I don't know about any of that stuff."

"Hot fudge volcanoes?"

"Nope."

"Streets paved with Astroturf?"

"Nope."

"The hit-song idea book?"

"What?"

"You're not cooperating," Mara yelled. She stalked to the record player and lifted the needle, making a terrible ripping sound. The clanking and creaking and moaning stopped abruptly. She turned, pointed at him and said, "The containment field is holding you in a Tuolumne toaster."

"Grubber won't like this."

"Grubber can suck vacuum. When I turn on the toaster, it will jam every electrochemical impulse in your brain, and your intelligence will drop to the level of a mushroom." She waited expectantly.

Rodney frowned but said nothing. He was terribly frightened even as he tried to convince himself that there were worse ways to spend his life than as a fungus.

"The strong silent type, eh?" Mara snapped her fingers, and a cloud gathered before him at eye level. A three-dimensional image formed. It showed a green creature with six arms in much the same position as Rodney was now. A creature much like the one he'd defeated aboard *Daisy* pulled a lever on the side of the toaster, and the coils began to flash and spit lightning while they buzzed and crackled. The eyes of the green creature rolled and then it screamed.

Mara snapped her fingers again and the cloud broke up, taking the image with it. "Instant mushroom soup," Mara said with a delight that made Rodney squirm.

"I'm not just being brave," Rodney cried. "I really don't know any of that stuff. Earth isn't the Legendary Treasure Planet. If there was a fudge volcano on Earth, I'd have heard about it."

"You can't be telling the truth. Obviously Grubber

Young told me the Earth isn't the Legendary Treasure Planet because it *is*. Or maybe it isn't, after all. That would be just like Grubber, telling me it isn't because it really isn't. Then when I go to investigate, he and Drum are off to the *real* Legendary Treasure Planet." Mara considered the possibilities.

Rodney was losing track of Mara's arguments. He was also tired of being a prisoner. There seemed to be no way out. But maybe, he thought as he looked up at the light bulb, there was a way in. Cautiously, Rodney lowered his arms. It was like moving through molasses, but not impossible.

"What are you doing?" Mara said.

"Preparing to blow my nose. It's an old Earth custom."

"So you are from Earth!" she cried.

"Well, yeah. I told you I was."

Rodney felt around in his pockets and found a big pill of ancient Kleenex. He began to open it into a usable, if wrinkled and disgusting, sheet.

"What about the *Woman Flagging Down a Bus?*"

Rodney nodded. As he had hoped, the force field actually pulled his hand in the proper direction. Mara watched him closely while he quickly reached up and gripped the hot light bulb with the Kleenex. "What are you doing?" she cried.

The force field produced by the light bulb was designed to prevent him from escaping—which was to say, from moving outward. The designers had never expected anyone to attempt moving inward—which was to say, toward the light bulb. Rodney attempted to turn the bulb, and it moved. He kept turning.

In the fateful moment during which Mara ran toward him, Rodney unscrewed the light bulb far enough that the light went out. He leaped from the Tuolumne toaster and faced Mara in a martial-arts crouch. "I am obligated to warn you my hands are licensed as deadly weapons," he said.

"Don't shoot!" Mara cried.

The fact that his hands might fire something was a new idea for Rodney, and of course entirely wrong. Still, he was not above taking advantage of Mara's misconception. While he pointed a finger at Mara like a kid playing cowboys and Indians, he used his other hand to reach into the toaster and screw in the light bulb. When it came on, the light sucked at his arm as if it were a tar pit. Rodney was able to pull his arm out, but slowly. Evidently, the restraining field could not keep him inside if part of him was outside.

When Rodney was free he said, "Get into that toaster."

Glaring at him, Mara stepped in among the springs.

Still covering her with his finger, Rodney backed into the tall grass. He turned and ran and almost slammed into a wall made of wooden boards. A sign in Mobambi said "Bar" and pointed a tentacle. He followed the sign to a heavy door and entered Finigle's Last Chance Bar. The torture chamber was just one more Earth exhibit.

A little light-headed, Rodney ran back to his room and sat on his feather, breathing hard. Drum was busy under the card-making machine. Since he had opened the first letter from Grubber Young and Drum, unpleasant and inconvenient things had happened to Rodney. Only in repose could these dangerous events be considered adventures.

Each time one of these terrible things had happened he'd been scared but he had, in Waldo's words, "handled it." In fact, he'd discovered that cheating disaster gave him a certain euphoria. No wonder his parents had such fond memories of their own adventures. Rodney was curious to see how long he could keep this up. After all, he hadn't saved a planet yet.

Drum came out from under her card-making machine and asked Rodney what was wrong.

What would be the heroic thing to say? "Nothing," Rodney said. "I just had a little talk with Mara."

"What did you tell her?"

"I tried the truth, but she wasn't satisfied."

"She wouldn't be. She's been dealing with Grubber too long." Drum thought for a moment and said,

"And she's a lot more dangerous and relentless than Grubber thinks. After this little episode, her techniques will become more drastic."

"I can handle it," Rodney said with more confidence than he felt.

"Maybe. Maybe it's time you went home."

"No."

Drum shrugged and said, "Suit yourself." She went back under the card-making machine.

Despite Rodney's outward calmness, he thought staying out of Mara's way for a while might be a good idea. She was likely to be pretty hot about his escape. He found his kazoo and said, "I'm going to find a place to play."

Rodney hurried out to the hallway with the kazoo case under his arm. Waiting for the elevator was a long, difficult time. When the elevator came at last, Rodney went down to the tunnel entrance to the Planetoid of Amazement and along it to the *Cosmic Ray*.

He plunked himself down into the acceleration couch where he'd spent most of the six days out from Earth, and took his kazoo from its case. The instrument felt good in his hands. He played scales for a while and then played as much of the hair-cutting scene from Pastrami's *Samson and Delilah* as he could remember. It sounded fine now, of course. He wished he'd thought to bring some sheet music; he'd never been good at memorizing. For a while he just sat with the kazoo in his hands, not really thinking at all. Someone clumped up the stairs outside the ship. There was a good chance it was Mara or Grits, looking for him. Rodney grabbed his kazoo and its case and ran into the kitchen, now the engine room, of the *Cosmic Ray*. He crouched against the wall with his kazoo against his chest, waiting to see what would happen next.

17

Monsters from the Sid

The airlock cycled open, and to Rodney's surprise and relief, it was not Mara but Grubber Young and Drum who came in. Rodney's first impulse was to leap up and greet them, but he thought better of it. He might learn something interesting if he stayed hidden.

"Here we are," Grubber said. "Now what?"

"Trust me another minute," Drum said. Rodney heard the two of them moving around the ship, but he had no idea what they were doing.

"Never trust a being who says trust me," Grubber said and laughed nervously. A moment later he said, "What are you doing with that blue card! Wait!" The moving was more frantic. Then the voice of the blue-carpet creature said, "Welcome aboard your Starship Club emergency ship. Our records show that you have already reached your primary destination. Further use of this ship will be charged to your account at our regular rates for time and mileage. Tap card once to abort. Tap card twice to continue."

"Wait!" Grubber cried again, but the end of the word was lost in the roar of rocket wash.

Rodney was thrown against a wall and held there. This was great! Drum had just abducted all of them aboard the *Cosmic Ray*, an event that smacked of big-time adventure. Better yet, it seemed to have nothing to do with the increasingly nasty Mara or her search for the Legendary Treasure Planet. Rodney might save a planet yet!

The roar faded to the distant familiar drone. Rodney was able to move again, and he stood up. He was aboard the ship and part of the adventure now, for better or worse.

Both Grubber and Drum were on the deck, probably thrown there by the force of the takeoff. Drum was shaking her head as if to clear it, and Grubber looked angry enough to chew off his own leg. He shouted, "That's it, Drum. You're fired!"

Drum pulled herself to an acceleration couch and said casually, "That's okay, Grubber. I won't be able to stay with you any longer anyway."

"What?" said Grubber.

"What?" said Rodney.

They both looked up at Rodney. He was framed by the engine-room window.

"What are you doing here?" Drum said.

"I came out here to play my kazoo. What are *you* doing here?" He and Grubber watched Drum expectantly.

Drum checked readings on the control board, leaned back in her acceleration couch, and said, "I'm a secret agent from Timbuck Two and I'm on my way out there, thataway, to the Sid." She pointed at the forward bulkhead and beyond.

"Why?" Grubber said. But before Drum could speak, he stood up and said, "On the other hand, wait a minute. While you're back there, Rodney, make up three burgers. I'll get the chocolate shakes. I think this is going to be a long story."

They eventually settled around one of the few tables that was still a table and Drum said, "The Sid is the home star system of the Slignathi, the scourge of the universe. My assignment is to go there, seek out the Slignathi, and destroy them."

"Slignathi?" Rodney said excitedly. "Sure, the big evil thing. From the yellow sticker I knew it had to be something like that."

Grubber shook his head. "But the Slignathi are just a fable. They aren't real. They don't exist."

"We on Timbuck Two discovered otherwise." Drum walked to the control board and made adjustments. Section after section of the sky wavered on the main viewscreen until she found the one she wanted. She pointed to a constellation that looked vaguely like a cockeyed face and said, "This is Herbert the Smirker, a constellation that can be seen from

Timbuck Two. The Sid is right here." Drum pointed to a star at one end of the crooked mouth.

Rodney felt uneasy. If he could trust Drum's feelings, the Slignathi were even nastier than Mara at her worst.

Grubber said, "For someone with a mission, you spent a long time on Hutzenklutz Station."

"It became necessary," Drum said. "Years ago I was on my way to the Sid when my ship broke down on Way Out Three."

"I remember Way Out Three," Grubber Young said. "It's a nasty hole."

"That's for sure," Drum said. "More important, nobody there knew how to fix my ship. Just to get away from there and hoping for the best, I hired on with you."

Grubber looked away, into the past, and said "I remember you offered me a Timbucker ship as evidence you were a good finder. That was your own ship, wasn't it?"

"Guilty. The *Ship of Amazement* hauled it home and it's still on exhibit."

Excitedly, Rodney said, "That was the ship where you got the blue cracker."

Drum nodded.

Grubber said, "I know for a fact that a few of the ships out in the Parade of Ships of All Planets can fly. The *Ship of Amazement* certainly could. Even Grits' ship, the *Daisy*, could fly before it blew up. Long be-

188

fore now you could have gone to the Sid aboard one of them."

"But not one of the navigational computers aboard those ships knows the Sid's location. I know; I checked. And though I had the navigational chips I took from my own ship, I didn't know how to transfer the information from them to some other ship. However, following the step-by-step instructions in those Starship Club magazines you've been tossing into my room for years, I was able to rewrite the navigation code used by my ship's computer so it could be used by a Starship Club rescue ship."

Rodney swallowed the bit of burger he'd been chewing and said, "That's why you acted so strange when you saw the *Cosmic Ray*. You knew you could go to the Sid aboard it."

"Right," said Drum. "I was finishing my calculations on our way back to Hutzenklutz Station from Earth. Then, during Rodney's tour of the Parade of Ships of All Planets, I copied the final version of my navigational program from my old Timbucker ship onto one of these oodles"—she held up a blue plastic cracker— "so called because it can carry oodles of information. I had no problem loading the program into the *Cosmic Ray*'s navigational computer."

Rodney said, "You were lucky that Grits' ship blew up and he came after us. Without that, you'd have just gone back to Hutzenklutz Station aboard the *Ship of Amazement* instead of aboard the *Cosmic Ray*."

"It wasn't exactly an accident." Drum looked hard at Rodney.

Rodney thought for a moment and snapped his fingers—which seemed to impress Drum. "It was that extra thing you asked me to do with the kazoo, wasn't it?"

"The noise made bubbles in the *Daisy*'s fuel line. *Kablooey!*" She opened out her hands into an explosion.

"You almost killed Grits."

"He almost killed us, remember?"

Grits' attack on his parents' house seemed like ancient history. Rodney said, "I guess adventures get complicated."

"Let's just say I'm very serious about my job." She shook her head. "And I didn't expect to have you along in the *Cosmic Ray* either last time or this."

Rodney said, "That's okay." He smiled and said, "It's my adventure as much as yours." He gave Drum a friendly punch in the shoulder.

Grubber Young shook his head. "Don't try to kid a kidder, Drum. We see a Starship Club emergency ship every so often. The *Cosmic Ray* wasn't the first."

"What would have been your reaction if I'd said I wanted to fly off somewhere in one of those emergency ships?"

"Depends on what your reasons were."

"Suppose I said you had to trust me?"

"Slignathi, Drum—" Grubber stopped himself, looked a little embarrassed, and said, "Great Frooth, Drum! You could have told me what was going on! You *should* have told me! You'd have been off and doing long ago."

Drum smiled shyly and said, "Anybody could be a Slignathi or one of their agents. You never know."

"You don't trust me?" Grubber said, shocked.

"I trust your good intentions. But what you didn't know, the Slignathi or their agents couldn't torture out of you. Now that we're on our way, nothing you could tell them matters."

Grubber thought about that and looked more and more frightened all the time.

Drum said, "Besides, these ships don't fly by themselves, you know, despite the fact they always know where they're going. This way you can fly the *Cosmic Ray* back to Hutzenklutz Station. It'll make a swell exhibit."

Grubber Young slowly regained his composure. Feigning a lightness Rodney was certain he did not feel, Grubber said appreciatively, "Got it all worked out, don't you, kid?"

Drum shook her head and sucked at her chocolate shake. She said, "Not as much as I'd like. I know where the Slignathi are. I have a ship to get me there. I'm just not sure I can handle what happens next."

"That's great," Rodney cried.

Drum and Grubber looked at him as if he'd lost his mind. Grubber said, "It is?"

"Sure. Ever since you guys made contact with me, I've been worried about my ability to handle a really big adventure. It's kind of nice to know that the professionals worry about the same stuff."

Drum grinned and punched Rodney in the shoulder. They hooked fingers all around.

Though they were in transit for a few days, the blue-carpet creature did not advertise at them as it had done on the way from Earth. It was also a pleasure not to worry about Drum. She joined them at meals and in games against the computer and was jolly enough. But at odd moments Rodney caught her staring at the main viewscreen, contemplating the star growing there. He and Grubber did it too.

Rodney was determined that they would all handle the situation together. He brought up the Slignathi whenever he could and made it their main topic of conversation. Wanting to leave nothing to chance, they discussed every point of Drum's plan.

They were only a few days out from Hutzenklutz Station when a strange voice bellowed in Mobambi, "Attention Slignathi Armada. This is the Grand

192

Pregnestic speaking."

"What is it?" Rodney cried.

"Shush!" Grubber and Drum said together.

The bellowing voice went on: "Immediately change course for planet Earth, the Legendary Treasure Planet. Coordinates are being sent to your navigational computers *now*. That is all." A loud click made Rodney's head hurt.

Sounding upset, Grubber said, "It looks as if we don't have to find the Slignathi. They found us."

"I don't think so," Drum said. "That transmission wasn't meant for us. It was meant for the Slignathi Armada."

"They're going to the Earth," Rodney said grimly. "We have to do something."

"Not much we can do against an entire armada," Grubber said. "These Starship Club ships aren't armed with so much as a pocketknife."

Rodney knew Grubber was right. Yet just giving up was not acceptable. He said, "What do you say, Drum?"

"I say the Sid can wait. We're on our way to Earth." She began to make adjustments on the control panel. "Or as the Starship Club computer calls it, Planet 5276-W."

Seconds later, acceleration pushed Rodney back in his chair.

18

The *Destruction Derby*

Once, while on the way to Earth, Rodney had a terrible dream. He awoke thrashing around, fighting off nightmare versions of Mara and Grits. Across the room Grubber and Drum were sharing a burger. Rodney fell asleep watching them. This time he slept soundly.

After a little over a standard week, the *Cosmic Ray* was approaching Earth. Rodney's home planet was the most beautiful thing he'd ever seen. The blue-carpet creature appeared in the space formerly occupied by the coffee urn and said, "We are now approaching Planet 5276-W. Please request manual control when ready."

"So where are the Slignathi?" Grubber said while the three of them looked at the main viewscreen. All it showed was the Earth, a field of stars, and a bit of the moon. Nothing showed up on dowsers either.

Grubber had gotten a lot cockier on their way to Earth and had just about convinced himself that Drum was wrong about the Slignathi, and that the message they'd intercepted was a malfunction or some kind of joke.

"Whose joke?" Drum asked, reasonably enough.

"I don't know," Grubber said in frustration. "You keep telling me it's a big universe. Somebody out in the universe has a peculiar sense of humor."

Drum was not convinced by Grubber's arguments, and neither was Rodney.

They had almost finished their first orbit when an alarm rang. "Is that them?" said Rodney as he and the others gathered at the main control board.

On the main viewscreen was a fleet of silver-trimmed black ships. The fleet was so large, the screen could not hold all of it. There might have been hundreds of ships or thousands. They looked alien and nasty, a little like bats, a little like spiders, as if designed to strike fear into the hearts (or whatever) of the greatest number of races.

"That's them," said Drum.

Rodney had a bad feeling about this.

The radio wasn't on, but suddenly a deep voice bellowed at them in Mobambi. Using the entire hull of the *Cosmic Ray* as a speaker, it said: "People of Earth! This is the Grand Pregnestic of the glorious Slignathi Armada. We are here to relieve your pitiful planet of its Legendary Treasures. Surrender or suffer the consequences!"

"Why did we get here first?" Rodney said, his voice shaking.

Drum frowned.

Grubber said, "The *Cosmic Ray* is a pretty fast ship. Maybe—"

"Maybe we've been had," Rodney said.

"Rodney's right," Drum said. "We were *supposed* to intercept that first transmission."

Grubber stared at the two of them, obviously putting facts together in his head. He said, "You mean we led them here?"

"That's my guess," Drum said.

"Well then, let's lead them away." One of his hands followed the other through the air.

"Somehow," said Drum morosely, "I don't think that would be very convincing."

"I suppose not," Grubber said.

"So we've been tricked!" Rodney said. "So what! Big deal! What are we going to do about it?"

After a moment Grubber and Drum nodded. Grubber took manual control of the *Cosmic Ray* and pulled back the throttle. The ship went dead in space relative to the Slignathi Armada and floated there, like a minnow confronting a cloud of sharks.

Rodney madly tried to think of something to say that would save his home planet. The Grand Pregnestic probably thought everybody in the universe spoke Mobambi. But nobody on Earth understood it, so they didn't even know they were under attack! What the Earthpeople did make of the incomprehensible voice booming from their walls and furniture, Rodney could not guess. While Rodney was thinking, the Slignathi, who evidently did not rate high on patience, fired multicolored beams at the Earth.

Grubber changed the viewscreen channel. He and Rodney and Drum watched with horror as the death beams struck the surface, kicking up house-size clods of dirt. The beams formed the center of swirling storm clouds, and rain began to fall in sheets. Lightning flashed. On another channel volcanoes spit up lava. On a third channel smog gathered into a dirty yellow pillow and smothered a city. They watched with morbid fascination.

"Surrender or die," the Grand Pregnestic cried.

"Let's see the Armada again," Rodney said. "There must be a way."

Grubber switched the channel and once more the Slignathi Armada filled the viewscreen.

"Really odd," Rodney said.

"What?" said Grubber.

He pointed at the screen. "Look at the way the Armada ripples where the edge of it dips into Earth's atmosphere."

"Almost as if the Armada isn't there at all," Drum said.

"Of course it's there," Grubber said.

"Maybe not." Rodney pointed again. "A movie would look like that if you tried to show it underwater."

"You think the Armada is a projection of some kind?"

Grubber said, "Dowsers don't say anything one way or another."

Rodney peered at the viewscreen and said, "What's that?" He pointed to a speck on the screen in the center of the Armada. Grubber made an adjustment, and the sector of the screen Rodney had pointed to sprang toward them.

The speck was now recognizable as a hat, a derby. Rodney said, "That looks like one of the emergency ships I saw in the Starship Club catalog."

"It's the *Destruction Derby*," Drum said with surprise.

"On dowsers too," Grubber said. "I don't believe it. Grits has been tinkering with the *Destruction Derby* for years."

"Believe it," Drum said. "The *Derby* must be the source of those death beams."

Rodney nodded as he smiled grimly. "My guess is that Mara and Grits are aboard."

"Unless the Slignathi and Mara have the same taste in vehicles," Grubber said. He shook his head and said, "I thought Mara was just a friendly competitor."

His head kept shaking. He found the evidence difficult to believe. "She *can't* be one of the Slignathi."

"Why not?" said Rodney.

Grubber had no answer. His faith in Mara and maybe in himself was gone. Rodney put a hand on his shoulder and said, "What matters is that the Slignathi Armada must be an illusion projected by Mara and Grits."

"What about the Grand Pregnestic?" Grubber said.

"More special effects," Rodney said. It was only a theory. How could he sound so certain? Maybe part of being a hero was running with your best theory instead of waiting for things to get worse.

"I don't think the weather down on Earth is an illusion," Drum said.

Grubber said, "I guess they don't want to beat up the planet too much. They don't want to hurt the Legendary Treasures."

"Lots of property damage though," Rodney said. His mind raced. It was up to them to save the planet. The *Destruction Derby* fired another burst of death beams. "Surrender or die!" the Grand Pregnestic cried.

"Let me at that radio," Rodney said. He took his kazoo from its case and held it ready. "Cover your ears, Drum."

"What are you going to do?" Grubber cried.

Eager to begin, Rodney said quickly, "I'm going to see if I can't put bubbles into the *Derby's* fuel line like I did to the *Daisy*. We'll blow them out of the sky with music!"

"What about us?" Grubber said calmly.

Drum nodded. "We have a fuel line too."

"Oh," said Rodney. He lowered his kazoo.

The Grand Pregnestic cried, "Give up your Legendary Treasures or we will exterminate you!"

"Good try," Drum said sadly.

"Surrender or die," the Grand Pregnestic bellowed.

"One-track mind," Grubber said.

"I have another idea," Rodney said. He switched on the radio again and said, "In the name of planet Earth, we aboard the *Cosmic Ray* surrender to the Grand Pregnestic and the Armada of the Slignathi."

Grubber slid the hush control into place and said, "Surrender? To Mara? Never."

"The *Destruction Derby* is a Starship Club emergency ship, isn't it?"

"How would I know?" Grubber shouted.

"It was in the catalog."

"What if it is, Rodney?" Drum said.

"Then I have a plan."

The rumble of the Grand Pregnestic's voice shook the hull when he said, "We accept your surrender. Prepare to be boarded."

"Now what?" Drum said.

Rodney smiled. His plan was already working. He said, "Now we put out the welcome mat."

"I don't get it," Grubber said.

"Point of view is everything. Don't think of Mara and Grits coming here to board us. Think of their coming here as our opportunity to capture them. And because the *Derby* is a Starship Club ship, it'll take only one of us to fly it back to Hutzenklutz Station. The other two can stay here and keep a close watch on the prisoners."

"*I'm* impressed," Drum said, and Grubber agreed.

On Grubber's order Drum inflated a pressure tunnel that would help connect the two ships. The *Destruction Derby*, with the Slignathi Armada spread out behind it like a fan, approached the *Cosmic Ray*.

19

This Side Up

Mara and Grits were attacking the Earth. Rodney was shocked that so large a crime could be committed by just two people. Of course he'd seen the Earth attacked in movies and books, but this was different. This was real. The horror of it was almost too big to comprehend. The Planetoid of Amazement was a great place, but it wasn't home and never would be. Only Earth was home and everything that went with it.

For over a week the *Destruction Derby* must have followed the *Cosmic Ray* just outside dowser range, which meant that, in addition to weapons and a 3-D projection system, Mara's ship also had better dowsers than the *Cosmic Ray*.

Rodney and the others watched while the main viewscreen showed them a pressure tunnel snaking out from the *Derby*; with a clang, its end automatically connected with the *Cosmic Ray*'s own. A moment later somebody was pounding on the outside of the *Cosmic Ray*'s main hatch.

"Everybody know what to do?" Rodney said. He

tried to appear calm, but inside, thoughts and emotions swirled around. He felt a little sick.

"You bet," Grubber said. In the last few minutes he'd become really excited about Rodney's plan. Evidently he was determined that Mara would pay for making a fool of him.

Drum opened the hatch, and Grits dropped in brandishing a ray gun. "All right," he said, "reach for the sky!" He chuckled at Rodney. "Nothing to fling at me this time, eh, whippersnapper?"

"Where's Mara?" Grubber said.

"Do we look stupid to you? She's guarding our ship." He smiled nastily. "It don't take more than one of me to take this ship away from you varmints."

Rodney hadn't expected that one of them would come alone. Grubber glanced worriedly at Rodney. Rodney thought fast and said, "Looks like they win the Legendary Treasure Planet fair and square."

"Yeah," said Grits. "Once we get *you* buckaroos and buckarettes out of the way." He waved the ray gun around in a manner Rodney thought was pretty careless.

"Don't shoot," said Rodney. "Look, we'll give you some burgers and fries if you don't hurt us."

"What's that?" said Grits, immediately suspicious.

"I don't know," said Grubber. "Do we want to give him any Legendary Treasures when Mara isn't here?"

Grits seemed to like the idea of getting first dibs on a Legendary Treasure. He said, "Don't worry about her. Enough to go around. What's burgersandfries?"

Promising to show him, they took Grits into the kitchen-turned-engine room, and Grubber started to make lunch. Grits tried to watch all three of them at once, but he was only one guy. "I'll get the salt!" Drum cried and ran around the room. "Onions!" Grubber cried. "I must have onions!"

"I'll get them," Rodney shouted, and ran from the room.

The tunnel had no artificial gravity, but Rodney ignored the queasy feeling in his stomach and the ringing in his ears as he pulled himself hand over hand to the *Destruction Derby*. He told himself that he had no time to be frightened of what he might find there. Grits was easily distracted, but he had a short attention span: How long would it take him to notice Rodney was gone? Rodney hoped by that time he'd have captured Mara somehow and taken control of her ship.

Fat chance. Rodney didn't want to die to save the Earth, but he knew by now that Drum was right. Adventures were frequently dangerous. He couldn't back out.

Rodney stopped himself at the end of the tunnel. He took note of where the floor and ceiling were, oriented himself, and stepped inside the *Derby*, where he immediately had weight again. The inside of the ship was one big room with concentric humps ringing its center like the circles on a bull's-eye. The room was dimly lit, much like Finigle's Last Chance Bar, and every surface was covered with silvery metal plate.

The control board stood against a wall and looked very much like the one back aboard the *Cosmic Ray*. The *Derby must* be a Starship Club emergency ship. Yet Rodney had difficulty imagining how the *Derby* had been disguised when Mara and Grits had picked it up.

Opposite the control board was a Tuolumne toaster. Evidently, Mara had not given up the idea of making him into an exhibit. Maybe she wanted to make all three of them exhibits.

Rodney had taken two steps toward the control board when Mara stopped him by saying, "Hold it right there, buster." Mara stepped out from behind the toaster and pointed a ray gun in his direction. "Well," she said, "here we all are at last."

"I keep telling you, Mara. Earth is not the Legendary Treasure Planet."

"So Grubber said. That's one of the reasons I don't believe you. Once you're out of the way, Grits and I can find out for ourselves." She leveled the ray gun at him and threw a big switch on the side of the toaster. Inside, coils and springs glowed as electric bolts jumped and snapped between them. She said, "Climb into that toaster."

Frightened, depressed, angry at himself for having made such a mess of things, Rodney walked slowly toward the machine wondering if he'd like being a mushroom. Mara's ray gun never wavered. He felt like a target at the wrong end of a shooting gallery. When he was close enough to the toaster for the electricity in the coils to make the hairs on his arms stand up, Rodney stopped.

"Go ahead," Mara said.

"No," said Rodney. "I don't want to be an exhibit. You'll have to kill me."

"You'll *like* being a mushroom," Mara said encouragingly.

Rodney waited a long moment, and then said, "Okay." He lifted his foot, but instead of stepping forward, he dropped to the deck and, breathing hard, crawled as fast as he could along the valley between two of the humps. The control board seemed to be miles away. Rodney took a deep breath and rolled over a hump. The ray gun made a *zoing!* and sparks flew near Rodney as a white beam ricocheted off the hump and made it hot. Mara fired twice more and cried out in agony. Something clattered into a corner. It might have been her ray gun.

Rodney took a chance and slowly lifted his head

high enough to see over the hump.

Mara stood there breathing hard, her hands balled into fists. She saw him and laughed in an ugly way. "No ray guns for you, buster. Only the best, the personal touch." Mara stretched both hands toward the ceiling while Rodney watched, more frightened than he had ever been.

Suddenly, Mara's skin ripped open, releasing a dead-mildew musk Rodney had smelled once before. She tore away her skin in shreds to reveal a blobby gray creature like the guard he'd met aboard the *Daisy*. The creature wore a uniform, parts of which seemed to be alive. Rodney shivered as it reached out at him with its long bony fingers.

"Surrender yourself to me and I will be merciful," Mara said in a voice much like the Grand Pregnestic's.

"You're a Slignathi!" Rodney cried.

"Yes," Mara hissed. "Grits and I are the last of our race. But we will survive long after you and your friends are gone." She flopped toward Rodney on her mammoth flippers. He moved away from her in the direction of the control board.

She moved to cut him off. They shuffled for a while, doing a sort of perverse dance. She would not allow him to get any closer to the control board than he already was.

Mara stopped, howled angrily, and said, "Of course,

mercy is no fun!" She laughed in a terrible way and attacked Rodney. At the same moment he made a desperate lunge at the control board, hooked his foot around the leg of an acceleration couch, and turned a dial.

With the gravity gone, Mara's leap sent her banging into the ceiling. Rodney shoved her toward the other side of the room. She screamed as she coasted, flailing around in the air. Rodney gently increased the gravity, and she crashed into the Tuolumne toaster. Her scream became a shriek that suddenly stopped. The echo of it rolled on, and then the silence was eerie.

Rodney turned the gravity back up to normal and went to look at Mara. When he turned off the toaster, she was breathing hard, but her face was slack. No intelligence was in it. Even so, Rodney was afraid of her. He had seen a dead rat once—fat and black and reeking with germs. Even dead it was a terrible thing. He felt that way about Mara.

He pulled himself back to the *Cosmic Ray* and found Grubber and Drum about to come after him. "What happened?" they all said at once.

"Mara and Grits are both Slignathi," Rodney said. "The last of their race."

"I hope they're the last," Grubber said. "What did you do with her?"

"She kind of fell into her Tuolumne toaster."

Grubber nodded and commented about what a great exhibit she would make. Drum nodded and said, "Those who live by the toaster will become exhibits the same way."

While Rodney had been gone, Grubber and Drum kept Grits so entertained that he actually started eating his burger and fries before he noticed that Rodney had not come back with the onions. As they'd hoped, the food had so distracted Grits that Drum was able to get the ray gun away from him. Grubber carried him screaming and kicking to an acceleration couch, where he strapped Grits in with the buckles out of reach. Grits sat there now, so angry he couldn't even swear at them. He just glared and snarled.

After contemplating Grits for a moment, Rodney said, "What will you do with him?"

"He can help us take care of Mara," Grubber said.

Rodney said, "He'd more likely murder you in your beds some fine night."

"I hate to disappoint you guys," said Drum, "but I'm taking him back to Timbuck Two to stand trial."

"Of course, of course," Grubber said solemnly.

"Consarned varmints!" Grits shouted, and snapped at Grubber's hand resting on the arm of the couch.

Grubber quickly pulled his hand away and said, "I guess that means this is good-bye." He held out his finger to Drum.

"Trying to get rid of me?" Drum said.

"No. I just thought—"

"Hey," said Drum, "these two are the last of the Slignathi. My job is done. I'll need another one. I thought maybe I'd stay on at the Planetoid of Amazement and run the bar. If it's okay with you."

Grubber and Drum beamed at each other and hooked fingers. Grubber said, "This is great! And the *Destruction Derby* will make a nice addition to the Parade of Ships of All Planets."

"No," said Rodney. "I have a better idea." He smiled. His idea was really too good.

20

Pretty Slick

Rodney was pleased and proud and ready to go home. Past ready. And he thought he owed Rocky Smith and his parents something more than a couple of Grubber Young's promises. He said, "Listen, Grubber, I want to take the *Destruction Derby* to Earth with me."

Rodney could not have surprised Grubber and Drum more if he'd admitted to being a Slignathi himself. "What will *you* do with it?" Grubber said.

"I'll give it to Rocky Smith and he can make a diner out of it. My parents can invest."

Grubber looked dubious, but Drum said, "Pretty slick. And when a Timbucker says 'Pretty slick,' it means something."

"The ship isn't mine, I guess," said Grubber sadly.

That seemed to settle the question. Rodney collected his kazoo and his jacket and swam through the tunnel with them. Grubber and Drum took the unresisting Mara in hand and stood at the entrance to the tunnel shuffling around nervously.

Rodney stood with them, also feeling a little self-conscious. They hooked fingers all around. Rodney said, "It's been wonderful."

"Your very own adventure."

"I like to think of it as *our* adventure," said Rodney, feeling good as he said it. "Check on me in a few weeks. School will be out and I'll need a summer job."

Grubber nodded. "And bring along some of that drink your parents gave us."

"Chocolatron."

They hooked fingers a last time, and Grubber pushed Mara into the tunnel. Drum punched Rodney in the shoulder and followed.

Rodney settled into the central acceleration couch and recalled the things Grubber had taught him about piloting a Starship Club emergency ship. First he turned on the viewscreen and took a final look at the *Cosmic Ray*. In a moment it blasted away and was lost among the stars. While he contemplated the star field, a great idea occurred to Rodney: He could bring home a souvenir for his parents. He smiled. They would like it a lot.

Rodney was delighted to find that he was no longer jealous of his parents. He found, to his surprise, that he had an interest in Captain Conquer and the Tuatara. He was certain his parents would be interested in the Planetoid of Amazement. Waldo would be pleased to hear he really had *handled it.*

Rodney had missed a couple weeks of school, but his parents would probably cover for him. Besides, the adventure had been as educational as anything he might have learned in books, and it had given him confidence. Catching up would not be difficult.

Using the aim-and-go method of piloting, Rodney found his city and cruised over it looking for damage the death rays might have done. But aside from the fact that the streets were wet, everything seemed to be normal. If Rodney kept the facts to himself, most Earthpeople would assume they'd just been having some strange weather. Strange weather could also help explain the Grand Prognostic's threats. If he was asked, Rodney would suggest that the sound that had rattled across the planet was some bizarre kind of thunder.

He clicked on the normal radio and got carrier hum. As far as he knew, only one receiver on Earth would be able to hear his message. He cleared his throat and said, "Rodney Congruent calling the Earth. Rodney Congruent calling the Earth." He waited for a long time and called again. Still no answer.

After a moment of thought, Rodney pulled the kazoo from its case. He began to play the Captain Conquer theme. The jaunty and heroic melody fit his mood perfectly.

Rodney was barely into the first chorus when his father's voice came on the air. "Rodney," he said with surprise, "is that you?"

"It's me, Dad. Are you talking on the Captain Conquer communicator?"

"What else?"

"I thought so. You always said it would still work if it received the right signal."

"Where are you calling from?"

"A spaceship, Dad. A real spaceship."

"Do you have a pilot's license, Rodney?"

"Hi, Mom. Listen: I'm aboard a spaceship that looks like a hat. I'm going to land where the *Cosmic Ray Diner* used to be. Maybe you guys could come out and give me a ride home."

"Of course," Mr. Congruent said. "I'm only sorry we weren't able to help you before this."

"Dad, I had to do it myself this time."

"This time?" Mrs. Congruent said. "Will there be another time?"

"I have a summer job," Rodney said, and chuckled.

"Just tell me one thing," Mr. Congruent said. "Was it a good adventure?"

"The best. I have a present for you guys and everything." Rodney knew his parents would like the present. For one thing, it would go with their decor. It was the ray gun knocked out of Mara's hand just before she broke out of her costume.

Rodney skimmed the *Destruction Derby* across the empty field and set the ship down over the depression where the *Cosmic Ray* had rested for years. A crowd was gathering, but that was all right. This was no secret invasion. It was the Homecoming of Amazement.